IN THE SKIES

BERLIN FRACTURED, BOOK 3

MARION KUMMEROW

IN THE SKIES, Berlin Fractured, Book 3

Marion Kummerow

ISBN Paperback: 978-3-948865-14-6

Cover Design by JD Smith Design

Cover photo:

Background - Public Domain

Girl - Shutterstock

https://creativecommons.org/licenses/by-sa/3.0/de/deed.en

READER GROUP

Marion's Reader Group

Sign up for my reader group to receive exclusive background information and be the first one to know when a new book is released.

http://kummerow.info/subscribe

1

ZARA

Berlin, Germany, May 1948

Zara leaned back in her seat, watching as the ruins of Berlin passed by. Every second the train took her farther away from the city she'd learned to fear, and nearer to her new job as housemaid for an American family at the Wiesbaden airbase.

She had never personally met her employers, but judging by the phone calls with Mr. and Mrs. Gardner, they seemed quite nice. And they came highly recommended by friends of hers.

"Aren't you sad to leave Berlin?" Laura, the roommate of one of Zara's best friends, asked. Laura was three years younger than Zara herself, and her signature feature was the long, blond braided hair. She always looked like the poster child of the *Bund Deutscher Mädel* – an organization Zara had been forced to attend for many years, but that had long ceased to exist.

"I am sad to leave my friends, but not to leave the city. After the Soviets occupied it, it never returned to being the place I once called my home."

"But you live in the American sector, they treat us well." Laura shook her head, her braids bouncing around her shoulders. Her looks were a stark contrast to Zara's, who had thick waist-long black hair and such pale skin, that people had compared her to Snow White ever since she was a child.

"As long as you're in Berlin, you can never get away from those damned Russians. It's like being in an oversized prison, since they have encircled the city like a monster squeezing you in his jaws."

Laura laughed. "You're being overly dramatic. Heinz always says they're not half bad."

Zara preferred not to rise to the bait. She didn't particularly like Laura's boyfriend Heinz, who was engaged in all kinds of shady activities, especially the smuggling of luxury foodstuffs. Of course, he liked the corrupt Russians who sold him Crimean champagne, Beluga caviar and the colorful matryoshka dolls.

"I'm glad to leave that pile of rubbish behind and start a new life in Wiesbaden, far away from any Russians." She looked out at the landscape passing by. Since they had cleared the city borders, the train picked up speed and would bring them within the next two hours to the inner-German border at Marienborn. She gave a small sigh, knowing the ever-present tension would only leave her body once they reached the British zone.

It had been a folly to return to Berlin after the war, and she'd paid bitterly for her sentimental decision to relocate. But it was where her family had lived all her life, before her father had moved them to the beautiful Austrian city of Linz. For three years now, she'd lived in constant fear of the Soviet soldiers. Zara shook her head. She refused to think of that time and all the horrible things that happened back then.

"...I'm so excited to see Göttingen. Heinz has told me it's

beautiful." Laura had kept talking while Zara was lost in her thoughts.

"I was there before the war, my mother dragged us to see all the cultural buildings and museums. It's a traditional town, dating back to the first millennium," Zara said.

Since travel permits were so hard to get, the train wasn't full and she and Laura had managed to find a compartment all to themselves. That would change once they passed the border, but for now she enjoyed the space and stretched out her long legs. "What are you doing in Göttingen, anyway?"

Laura sat up, a big smile crossing her face. "I'm running some errands for Heinz. Can you imagine, me going all by myself into the British zone?"

"It's rather exciting." Zara thought, but didn't say out loud, that Heinz probably wanted to avoid unwelcome questioning if he undertook the journey himself. Even though he posed as a respectable businessman, everyone knew the real nature of his dealings. Officially, the occupation powers in Berlin frowned upon black marketeers, but they enjoyed the perks too much. Heinz and his uncle, the owner of the famous Café de Paris, offered whatever money could buy to those who could pay for it, and the authorities never harassed him more than was needed to keep up appearances.

That was likely to be different in the British zone of Germany, far away from the mutual coexistence in the capital where everyone knew everyone else. She didn't care much for Heinz or Laura, but thanks to his connections, she had been able to buy tickets on a direct train that passed through the Soviet occupied zone without a single stop. And that was worth gold. Zara was glad she was going to leave all of this behind.

A screeching sound tore through the air and she grabbed her armrest to keep from sliding off the seat. Moments later, the train came to a full stop.

"What's going on?" She craned her head to get a glimpse

through the window, but couldn't see anything, except for a red light somewhere in the distance.

"Probably just a blocked track," Laura speculated. Damaged tracks were a frequent occurrence and it seemed to happen especially often on the routes of the direct trains, allowing the Soviets to needle the other Allies with little pinpricks here and there.

Zara involuntarily clutched her handbag tighter. Every additional minute she had to spend in Soviet territory seemed to increase the heavy weight pressing down on her lungs until she could barely breathe.

It felt like an eternity, but was probably only minutes later, when their compartment door opened and several Soviet soldiers strode inside, sternly looking at the two women.

Suppressing the nervous trembling of her limbs, Zara waited with bated breath to hear what the soldiers wanted. She cast a sideways glance at Laura, unfazed as always, casting a bright smile at them.

The two men wore the Soviet army uniform, one of them had the facial features of those born far in the east of his vast country, while the other one showed the classic pale and angular face that marked him out as a Russian from a mile away.

"Papers please!" the blond one said.

They weren't supposed to ask for papers, since they had checked the passengers already four times in Berlin, the first time upon buying the tickets, then when she and Laura entered the restricted passenger area at the station. Their papers were checked once again when they reached the platform and a last time just before departure when the Soviet soldiers had to leave the train, since it was supposed to travel without stopping until it reached Helmstedt in the British zone.

But it wouldn't do any good to refuse their orders. Zara kept the expression on her face blank, as she opened her purse and pulled out her identification, the travel permit and the ticket and handed them over to the solider who'd asked her, while Laura handed hers to the other man.

The soldier took Zara's papers and scrutinized them, as if searching for something. Her nervousness grew when he gave her the once-over. It felt as if he was undressing her, trying to see through her clothes not only onto her bare skin, but also inside her soul, trying to find whatever secret she might have hidden.

Despite the crawling spiders on her skin, she didn't move, sitting rigid under his scrutiny, while his eyes flicked back and forth between the photograph on her *Ausweis* and her person, as if to make sure she was actually the person she pretended to be.

Who on earth would pose as me, anyway? she thought, having difficulties not to laugh out loud.

He spoke to his colleague in Russian, nodding at her and handing him her papers. More frantic spiders crawled over Zara's skin and she considered whether it would be worth jumping out of the half-open window.

The smell of trouble descended over their compartment and took her breath away. But much to her relief the Asian-looking soldier, apparently superior to the blond one, gave a slight shake of his head and returned the papers to her without the slightest hint of an emotion.

Once again, her hatred for the Soviets had gotten the better of her and she'd let her imagination run wild. To make sure she wasn't losing her mind, she peered over at Laura, who was storing her papers in her purse, humming a low tune. How on earth could that girl be so ... oblivious ... to everything going on around her? Zara shrugged, relaxing against the backrest of her seat and staring at the door through which the two Soviet soldiers had just disappeared.

She waited for the telltale sound of the carriage doors closing, so the train could continue its journey. But the only sounds she heard were steps in the corridor and the sudden opening of their compartment door once again.

She jerked her head toward the entrance, wondering whether new passengers had been allowed to board the train and this was the reason for their unexpected halt. But, much to her dismay, two tall men dressed in Soviet military police uniforms entered the compartment.

What do they want now? Couldn't these thugs simply leave her in peace? Didn't they see she was about to leave their sphere of influence for good? Soon, neither she nor they would have to deal with each other ever again.

Her knuckles hurt and she glanced down at her hands clutching her handbag. She willed her fingers to relax and slowly the blood returned to her fingers. There was nothing to worry about.

Laura's elbow against her ribs returned Zara's attention to the men in front of her, who'd apparently commanded her to do something, and the older one now pinned her with a furious glare.

"Excuse me, I didn't understand your question," she said.

"Open your suitcase." His command sounded like the bark of a dog. Short, loud, and sharp. Most of all, it brooked no dissent. Not that she had entertained the idea of opposing the order of a Soviet official. After all, they were the occupiers and she was...nobody.

"Yes." She got up, towering above him by half a head, as she stretched out her legs and arms to reach for her suitcase in the overhead luggage rack. It was small and light, since she didn't own many possessions. A few changes of clothing, a picture of her with Marlene and Bruni, taken last summer, two books and her toiletries. Her entire life in one small suitcase.

He rummaged through her things, causing her stomach to lurch. There was nothing secret or forbidden in that suitcase, but it felt entirely awkward having a man search through her most intimate wearables. She resisted the urge to close her eyes and crossed her arms in front of her chest, jutting out her chin.

As anticipated, he didn't find anything of value or interest and she wanted to cry with joy when he threw the suitcase lid shut. But even as he turned around, his gaze stayed on her face and then travelled downward, where it stopped on the delicate silver necklace with a pendant around her neck.

"This is a very beautiful necklace, I need to see the purchase certificate," he declared after a thorough inspection that she was sure wasn't entirely confined to the medallion, but also to the bare skin on her neckline. She cursed herself for not wearing a turtleneck pullover, but it had been hot these past few days and she'd opted for a summery blouse with a décolleté big enough to reveal the necklace and the pendant.

"My godmother gave the medallion to me on my fifteenth birthday," she said, hoping he wouldn't notice the trembling in her voice.

"How convenient."

"It's true."

"I'm very sure it is stolen. Take it off," he ordered and waited for her to remove the necklace from her neck. His eyes lit up when his thick thumb stroked the smooth surface, and moments later the necklace disappeared into his pocket.

Zara gasped, but didn't dare to protest, despite being heart-broken, since this was her only memory of her godmother. She cast a helpless glance at Laura, who pretended not to notice anything out of the ordinary. Arguing with a Soviet officer intent on stealing valuables wouldn't change anything, except get her into trouble. The necklace was lost.

The policeman turned around to look at Laura and her suitcase, but before he could order her to open it, another officer appeared in the compartment door.

"What's the delay?" he said in Russian. Zara had learned

enough of the loathed oppressor's language in the past years to maintain a very simple conversation, but usually pretended not to understand.

The policeman seemed to defend himself and after a short exchange of words, he pulled out Zara's necklace and pointed an accusing finger at her. The cold hatred in his eyes made her shiver. "You have been pilfering and stealing German cultural property."

"Why, no! My godmother gave it to me ten years ago. In fact, he's the one stealing it!"

As soon as the words left her mouth she regretted them, because his face turned into an ugly grimace and he turned toward the officer. "Comrade, you won't believe an obscure German slut over a member of the Red Army."

He held out the necklace to his superior, who eyed it and then said to Zara, "You're under arrest for smuggling, pilfering and stealing."

When Zara, frozen in place by fear, didn't move immediately, he said impatiently, "The great Soviet Union is intent on protecting the cultural property of Germany and you will be tried for your crimes."

There was nothing she could do, except to send a helpless plea for help to Laura, who only shrugged, her eyes wide open in anguish. It was a cruel irony of fate, because Zara was sure Laura was the one actually smuggling things in her suitcase.

Zara followed the two policemen from the train, like a lamb being led to slaughter. She was innocent, but would anyone care about that little detail? Going by what she knew about the Soviet system, she guessed not.

She jumped from the steps of the carriage onto the embankment, where yet another officer was waiting to lead her to a dark gray vehicle. He shoved her into the backseat together with two men who looked like the criminal she was supposed to be.

The car started and turned eastward to a place she didn't know and probably didn't want to know about. Her only hope was that Laura would alert someone to come to her rescue. Although that was a very long shot.

Nobody gave a shit about the fate of a German civilian. Each power could do whatever they wanted in their zone, without the others interfering. Zara was at the mercy of the Soviets, arrested for the alleged crime of stealing her own necklace, now deemed German cultural property.

2

GLENN

G lenn was squinting his eyes against the sun and launched the basketball. It flew in a perfect arc and dropped through the basket with ease.

"Wow. How can you do this?" John asked him, awe-struck.

Glenn caught the ball and passed it on to his best friend's son. It was nice to be admired, even if only by a seven-year-old. "Plenty of practice. And it obviously helps to be tall. Now it's your turn."

They continued to run, pass, dribble and throw for another fifteen minutes, until Glenn's best friend Charles Gardner came into the garden of his villa. "Dinner is ready."

John put down the ball and raced into the villa faster than Glenn could blink, but Charles caught him by the shoulder and admonished him, "Wash your hands first, or your mother will be very angry."

"Is he always that fast?" Glenn asked.

Charles laughed. "Not where school is concerned, but say

the word food and he's the first one in line. This kid has a huge appetite."

"We were the same, don't you remember?"

"That was a long time ago. Although I guess you never changed," Charles teased his friend. They'd grown up together in the Midwest, had even joined up together, but Glenn had become a fighter pilot, while Charles was an army engineer.

Charles's wife Catherine peeked out of the door, carrying little Lisa on her hip and furrowing her brow at the sight of her dirt-covered son. "Good gracious, Glenn, what have you done with him?"

"Nothing." Glenn grinned at the woman and pretended to want to hug her.

"Get off me, you sweaty good-for-nothing," she protested, holding the baby like a shield between them. "And wash your hands before dinner."

"Yes ma'am!"

"And your face, too!" She sighed and turned toward her husband. "How come Glenn hasn't grown up one bit in all these years?"

Charles laughed and kissed his wife. "That's what everyone's puzzled about. Thirty-one years and still behaving like a rowdy teenager."

AFTER DINNER GLENN and Charles retreated into Charles's study. "How's life treating you in Oberpfaffenhofen?"

"Not bad," Glenn hedged, but since he'd never been able to hide anything from his friend, he shrugged. "It's kinda boring, really. Not much flying. We mostly hang out and party." He glanced toward the closed door. "Drinks, girls, you know..."

"I forgot." Charles chuckled. "I've been with Cath so long, I barely remember my wild days."

Glenn never understood why his friend had been in such a hurry to marry his high school sweetheart when there were so many willing girls out there. Not that Cath was a bad woman, she was fantastic, but tying yourself voluntarily to just one woman? Complete folly. Akin to deciding to only ever again fly one kind of aircraft. "Honestly, I don't know how you do it. Don't you ever get bored staying with the same woman?"

"Never."

"I would. I mean, where's the adventure when you know exactly what's waiting for you every night?" Glenn sighed. He was getting bored with the other sex, not because he'd tied himself to one woman, but because they were all interchangeable. Same thing, just with a different wrapping.

"That's because you haven't met the right one. It's difficult with the recent war and you stationed overseas and everything. Have you thought about asking to be demobilized?"

"Nah, I actually asked for a transfer to Korea. With the upcoming elections there and everything, they'll need pilots and maybe..." Glenn secretly hoped for another war, so his talents as a fighter pilot would be in demand again and he wouldn't have to languish away in boredom. Ober'huffin'puffin, as the men had nicknamed the airbase next to Munich, was nice, in a beautiful landscape, relatively undamaged from the war, but it was much too tranquil for his liking and he spent most of his time with some stupid theory stuff instead of being behind the yoke.

The door opened and Cath entered the study, carrying a tray with coffee and whiskey. She placed it on the table and then flopped down on the couch. "Uff. The kids are finally in bed. I never seem to have enough time to do all the chores."

"What happened to the new maid? Wasn't she supposed to start working with us already?" Charles asked.

"Yes, yesterday."

"And why isn't she here?"

"That's what I'm asking myself. She left Berlin two days ago." Cath shot her husband an indignant glare and Glenn felt the tension rising like mist on a chilly night. One more reason never to get married.

Since he was their guest for the weekend and would have to suffer if the bad mood prevailed, he jumped in to calm the waves, "Maybe she got held up. You know how bad the transport between Berlin and our zone is."

"She could at least have called." Cath's voice was pure venom and Glenn almost felt sorry for the missing housemaid. That girl would have a difficult start.

"Maybe she couldn't find a functioning public phone." Glenn wanted to tell Cath that she lived in a happy bubble in Wiesbaden, where barely a building had been destroyed during the war and which looked like any normal town back in the States. He wanted to tell her how lucky she was to live in an actual house and not in a heap of rubble like the people in bigger German cities. But a sideways glance and a quick shake of the head from Charles kept him silent. Apparently, this was not a topic he should discuss.

"I'd better get to sleep. Thanks for the fantastic dinner," he said and made his way to the adjacent guest room. Once in bed, he couldn't sleep for a long time as thoughts about his future kept him awake.

He didn't want to be bored to death with the easy peacetime job at the godforsaken airbase in Oberpfaffenhofen, but he also didn't want to be demobilized just yet, because there wasn't much for him to do back home. He wanted to fly. Day and night. Every day. There had to be a job for him somewhere, where he could do just that.

3

ZARA

Every cell of her body was numb with fear and when she looked down at her clutched fingers, they were almost translucent. For a moment she listened intently, surprised her heart was still beating regular and strong.

The car ride seemed to go on forever, without anyone uttering a single word. The monotony only worsened things, because it gave her time to let her imagination run wild with the most horrid speculations.

When she glanced out of the window, she noticed the change in scenery and suppressed a shocked gasp when she realized that they had returned to Berlin.

The entire incident had been more than strange and she racked her brain to find out what they could possibly want from her. Surely, the alleged stealing of a necklace wasn't a crime severe enough to justify being brought back to Berlin. A queasy feeling pooled deep in her gut, and with sudden clarity she knew that this was about something bigger. The necklace was just an excuse.

The revelation brought only a moment of respite, because when she grasped its significance, her skin was crawling and with every passing minute her anxiety skyrocketed. She tried to even her breath, telling herself that nothing bad had happened...after a few minutes it worked and she calmed down enough to massage some blood into her lifeless fingers. Until she recognized the borough of Hohenschönhausen.

If she hadn't been squeezed in between the two men on either side of her, who in turn were handcuffed to the seats in front of them, she would have jumped off the car.

Hohenschönhausen was the location of the notorious NKVD prison where the Soviet secret police kept and tortured their prisoners. The panic pressed all oxygen from her lungs, and Zara distantly wondered how she was even still alive without the ability to breathe. Nobody who'd been inside the walls of this sinister building had ever returned to tell the tale, but rumors abounded.

Even her friend, the cabaret singer Bruni, who usually stayed well away from politics and kept on good terms with members of all four occupying powers, had refused to acknowledge the existence of this place, as if denying it was there could make the gruesome stories whispered behind closed doors disappear.

Zara closed her eyes and sent a prayer to the heavens that they were not headed to the infamous place of horrors. When she opened them again, the car had stopped in front of a large gate.

The sentry exchanged a few phrases with the policemen in her car and papers, including hers, were checked before he let the vehicle pass. They drove along past a large, low brick building, until they finally parked in front of a staircase.

Recognition hit hard when she spied the former canteen kitchen of the *Volkswohlfahrt,* the Nazi Social Welfare Service that had been requisitioned by the Soviets in May 1945 and transformed into a collection and transit camp for up to twenty thousand prisoners.

Everyone suspected to be a spy, terrorist, NSDAP official, or member of the Nazi police force, had been taken here to await their fate. But also, any and all persons deemed *hostile to the Soviet Union* could be sent here, and that included those people who criticized the communist regime, foremost journalists, radio reporters or members of opposing political parties. And now apparently people who were accused of stealing a silver necklace. She would have laughed if the circumstances weren't so dire. Being brought to Hohenschönhausen prison was something you wouldn't wish on your worst enemy.

From the outside, the huge brick building looked nice enough, with plenty of space and signs that indicated offices for Soviet officials. Zara scolded herself for being overly pessimistic. They would soon find out this was a huge misunderstanding and let her go free.

She willed herself to take a deep breath and relax her cramping muscles. The back door of the car opened and the burly, vicious-looking man sitting beside her was uncuffed and shoved out of the vehicle. Looking at his bull's neck, she decided her biggest worry right now was the danger of being locked up in a cell together with him.

Then it was her turn to be hauled from the car and she stumbled, almost falling flat on her face. None of the Soviet officers came to her help, but the awful-looking criminal stretched out his arm to steady her, showing half-rotten teeth in something that might have been an encouraging smile.

The other prisoner followed and the three of them were shoved into a huge hallway that was being cleaned by several women, who didn't even raise their heads to look at the newcomers, but kept sweeping the floor.

Zara swallowed and kept her eyes trained on the back of the man walking in front of her, determined to keep a positive attitude and not let herself get scared witless.

The officer leading their small group opened a heavy iron door that gave a bone-chilling creak, and then led them down the stairs into the basement. Zara instantly forgot all about being cheerful. Thick fear was creeping into her bones, like the chilly humid cold in the Austrian winters had done, and she shivered.

For a moment she forgot about her current predicament. Stepping into the cold, moldy air filled with anguish brought back memories she'd buried deep inside.

During the time her family had lived in the beautiful Austrian town of Linz, she'd only once visited the Mauthausen concentration camp that her father had commanded.

Usually her mother wouldn't let her get near the place, but that one time, there had been some important guests – Zara couldn't remember who it was – and her father wanted to show off his beautiful wife and daughter.

Zara was sixteen back then, and the images of the emaciated prisoners had shocked her to the core despite her father's assurances that they were all enemies of the Reich and deserved their treatment. The awful scene had instantly impressed itself on her soul and remained there ever since.

But she'd run away before meeting the important visitor and henceforward had refused to ever set foot in that ugly place again. Of course, she'd received a heavy beating at her father's hands for embarrassing him in such a manner in front of half the Nazi party, but the things she'd seen had distressed her too much to care about the physical punishment. As long as he didn't force her to go there ever again, she'd gladly receive every leather belt stroke he doled out.

A rough shove against her back brought her into the

present and she widened her eyes in shock at the sight unfolding in front of her. The basement, in hushed whispers given the sobriquet *U-Boot*, submarine, was a long hallway made of concrete with bright light bulbs hanging from the ceiling.

Left and right she saw metal doors with huge bolts. All of them were closed, except the last three at the end of the corridor, taunting her to dare and enter. Her steps slowed down and everything inside her wanted to scream and run away, but the officer next to her had anticipated her futile attempt and pushed the barrel of his gun between her shoulder blades, just as she heard the screeching sound of the basement door being locked and bolted.

Her fellow prisoners were shoved into the two cells to the right and the door slammed shut behind them, making Zara jump when the bolt was put in place with an odd sound of finality.

She felt as if she were suffocating and, within moments, her body was covered in goosebumps from head to toe. Without thinking, she instinctively turned around and ran, only to bump into the Soviet officer walking behind her. He gave an ugly leer, pressing her tighter against his body.

Her breath hitched in her lungs when she became aware of the growing bulge below his waist and she frantically struggled to get away from him. Moments later she found herself flung on the cold concrete floor of an empty cell, and the dull clacking sound from the other side of the metal door indicating that she was trapped.

Still reeling from the impact of falling to the ground, she came to her knees and looked around. The clammy cell was equipped with a bare wooden cot on one side and a bucket kitty-corner. From the ceiling hung the same sort of overly bright light bulb she'd seen in the corridor.

No windows. No sounds. No nothing. She crawled to the

door and pressed her ear against it, but couldn't hear anything, not even the retreating steps of her captors. She slunk to the floor, desperately alone, when suddenly pitiful moaning and wheezing cut through the eerie silence. Zara looked around the cell, but there wasn't a human soul there except for herself.

4

GLENN

The instructor pointed with the chalk in his hand at the class and said, "Who can tell us the advantages of the new radio technology?"

Glenn instinctively shrank in his seat, while his eyes were pinned to the blackboard. Some bright boy up in the hierarchy had had the brilliant idea to send all pilots on the airbase back to school.

All week they'd been stuck in this classroom repeating airplane maneuvers ad nauseam. Who cared about the theories behind doing flips and rolls when they weren't allowed to go up into the sky and actually perform them?

At least today they'd turned to something more interesting. Ground controlled approach. Glenn was still torn as to whether he liked the new technology or not. On the one hand it would take a lot of the creativity and freedom from flying. He had become a pilot to fly, not to let some blockheaded lad in the tower talk him to the ground. But on the other hand, landing by sight was not always possible and, in such instances, ground controlled approach, or GCA, would be a great help.

In the autumn fog over England during the war, he'd often had less than ideal weather conditions to land his fighter and would have been grateful for any help he could get from the ground.

But while he appreciated the added security during bad weather, he feared these penny-pinching bureaucrats would plan that one day the aircraft might fly entirely on autopilot, making the crew obsolete.

Gordon, the grind of the base, jumped up and answered the question. Glenn didn't listen. He really had better things to do with his life than to rehash the theory of radio waves and what-not. He looked out of the window onto the soft rolling hills of the Bavarian landscape. On clear days like today you could see the white-capped Alps and Germany's highest mountain, the Zugspitze, in the distance.

His mind was running off, planning to take a Cessna on a leisurely flight to the Alps and beyond, into Austria. It would be such a great trip: interesting and diverting. He wouldn't fly at the recommended height of seven thousand feet to evade all the high peaks, but would take her down low, enjoying the beautiful sights as he wound his way along the alpine streams and gorges.

He'd done this trip many times in his mind and with a finger on a map, but had unfortunately never found the opportunity to do the real thing. While the instructor droned on about wavelengths and radio transmitters, he thought back to the war, when his life had been exciting and adventurous.

It wasn't that he missed the constant danger of being shot down – he wasn't that crazy – but he missed the action, the adrenaline, the recognition. Soon, his mind was back years in the past, chasing a German Messerschmidt in a daring dogfight, drawing on every ounce of expertise behind the yoke he held.

He missed the time when he'd taken out his trusted bird on a daily basis. Nowadays the best he could hope for was a training flight once in a while. The military had even retrained him in flying clumsy C-47 Skytrains. Flying cargo machines! It was an insult to his abilities.

After the class, his commanding officer approached him. "Hey, Davidson. I need a volunteer for an urgent operation."

Urgent sounded adventurous. Glenn didn't even have to ask what it was. Anything would be better than another day of staring at endless chalk marks on a blackboard.

He offered himself up. "Sir, I can do it."

The officer pursed his lips. "I know you're bored here, but don't you at least want to know what it is, before you agree?"

"No, sir. If you thought of asking me, I'm sure I can complete the mission."

"Okay. Hop on the flight to Frankfurt leaving in forty-five minutes. There you'll be briefed."

That was rather mysterious, and Glenn asked, "Any more information?"

"No. Except that you might be away for a few days, so pack your duffle bag."

"Yes, sir." Glenn trotted off and stuffed his belonging into his kitbag. He didn't really care where he was going or how long he would be gone for, as long as the new mission involved flying. A doubt stabbed him. What if it didn't have anything to do with flying? His CO hadn't said. He shrugged. It was too late anyway, since he'd already volunteered.

In Frankfurt, he received orders to present himself at the flight office. He sauntered inside, his kitbag slung over his shoulder when he stopped dead in his tracks.

"Our pilot has arrived," General Harris, the commander of Berlin, said.

"Sir?" Glenn's eyes darted around the room. Apart from

Harris, there were three men he didn't know. Harris introduced them as the crew for this flight.

"I was told you're the best pilot we currently have in Germany and can land a fully packed C-47 under the worst conditions without breaking a sweat."

"I can." Glenn felt flattered, although the whole operation was more than strange. Since nobody offered any other explanation, he asked, "Sir, may I ask exactly what is expected of me?"

"You'll be informed strictly on a need to know basis. Suffice to know for now that you're flying us to Berlin and will stay there for the time being," Harris said.

Glenn closed his mouth, which was hanging agape. Did these people want to pull his leg? In his entire military career, he'd never had a stranger briefing, and he had participated in more than one cloak-and-dagger operation. He decided to ignore their secrecy and stuck to purely technical questions about flight time, weather conditions and his crew.

Less than an hour later he sat behind the yoke of the slow and plump cargo plane, still not quite grasping what was going on. He'd caught a glimpse of the cargo during the boarding and seen the words "Fragile. Glass " stamped on several of the boxes. They looked a lot like liquor crates, but who would organize a top-secret mission for alcohol? Maybe they were organizing some smashing surprise party for a big shot? Glenn scratched his chin and decided it was none of his business. As long as he was in the air, he was happy.

He'd never been to Berlin and when they entered the airspace over the city, he involuntarily held his breath. Three years after the war, all he could see was ruins. What a depressing place to live. How much nicer it was in Wiesbaden or even in boring Oberpfaffenhofen. For a fleeting moment the Gardners' new maid crossed his mind. No wonder she wanted to get away from here. Once he returned to Frankfurt he'd ask for permission to spend the night at his friend's place.

He touched down nice and smooth at Tempelhof Airport and left the cockpit to venture into the hangar and have a look at the precious cargo he'd just transported, but he was held back by some fresh-faced airport staff.

"Captain, if you will come with me please?"

Glenn shrugged. He might get a chance to have a look later. For the moment he followed the soldier through the long corridors of the airport building, all the way up to the eighth floor, until they arrived at the office of the airport commander.

The soldier knocked on the door and then said to the man inside, "Sir, Captain Davidson is here."

The commander got up and looked Glenn up and down. "I just received notice that you're going to be staying at the garrison for the next few days."

That was news to Glenn.

"I really wish they had given me this information earlier. Do they think I have nothing better to do than organize transport and accommodation on a whim?"

Glenn's eyebrows shot up. Not even the airport commander seemed to be privy to the true nature of this operation. What could be so important about a bunch of liquor crates?

The commander made a few calls and then said, "I've announced you at headquarters, and you are to stay in the guest barracks. At twenty hours there's a transport going there. Do you need anything else?"

Glenn didn't have to look at his watch to know that this was three hours away. Now that the excitement and exhilaration had worn off, he realized that he hadn't eaten anything since breakfast, except for a quick cup of coffee and a donut during his short stay in Frankfurt. "A bite to eat would be nice."

"Now, that's not a problem." The commander looked mollified. "Private Tenner will show you the break room, where you can grab something."

Glenn thanked the commander and followed Private Tenner from the room. Again, they walked through long corridors and three flights down to the fifth floor. Glenn had only ever been in the hangar and the passenger terminal and was quite surprised how huge the complex actually was.

It was a stark reminder of the Nazi megalomania and self-dramatization, the world's biggest airport for the future world-capital Germania. He scoffed. Thankfully it had never come to that. But even Glenn had to agree that Tempelhof Airport was unique. As far as he knew there wasn't anything similar to this magnificent structure anywhere in the world.

Even from the elliptical airfield, it was an impressive sight: the arched line of hangars stretching out for almost a mile, flanked by two office wings on either side. But the Nazis had not only surpassed everyone else with their boastful architecture, they'd also implemented cutting edge technology and processes. This was the only airport worldwide where the hangars, the passenger terminal and the administrative buildings formed one single and monumental complex.

They had also implemented a fantastic process for civilian, and in effect military, aviation, by meticulously separating passengers from cargo. Passengers didn't walk with their luggage on board by themselves, but the cargo was completely separated and handled by specialized cargo employees.

Glenn's eyes almost popped out as Private Tenner opened the door to the break area. The first thing he saw in the ballroom-sized room was a bowling alley.

"That's not for real, right?"

Private Tenner grinned. "It is. During breaks we can play here, or watch a movie over there." He pointed to the area on the far end with pool tables, a television set and several couches. "The canteen is over there. It's self service."

Glenn's gaze followed Tenner's hand and saw several serving trolleys filled with sandwiches, donuts, and thermos bottles with coffee. "Just what I need. Thanks."

Private Tenner warned him to be on time for the troop transport back to the garrison and then left him to his own devices. Glenn grabbed a few sandwiches and decided to flop onto one of the couches to get some shuteye. Since he was stuck in Berlin he intended to make full use of his unexpected free time and find out firsthand whether the Berlin girls lived up to their reputation.

He was awoken by some turmoil and opened his eyes to see several guys walking past in sports clothing with a basketball. Seeing someone about to engage in his favorite sport, Glenn shot up and asked, "Hey, you going to play somewhere?"

One of the men looked at him, "Yeah. Over there. You new?"

"Not new, stranded. Just flew in and got an unexpected leave."

"Lucky man. You up for a game?"

"Sure." Glenn agreed, before glancing down at his uniform. "I'll have to change, though."

"No probs. There's a locker room in the basketball hall."

Glenn was sure the other man was pulling his leg. Where on earth would they go to a real basketball hall, locker rooms included? But nevertheless, he grabbed his kitbag and followed them through another door.

"Wow!" was all he could say, as he stopped in his tracks, taking in the sight. A perfect basketball court, complete with professional baskets and floor markings, filled the hall, which was even bigger than the recreation area with the bowling alley. In contrast to the meager amenities they had in Oberpfaffen-hofen, these guys here lived in paradise.

He quickly changed into shorts and a shirt and forty-five minutes later, he was dripping with sweat, completely exhausted, but happy. What a great start to a few days on the prowl in the German capital.

On the way to the barracks his new friends filled him in on the best nightclubs in the cities and where to find the most beautiful girls. The unanimous opinion was that the famous cabaret Café de Paris was the place to go for someone who was only in town for a short time.

5

ZARA

The door opened and two Soviet officers in impeccable uniforms without a single crease walked in. One of them identified himself as Captain Grusow. He was exceptionally polite and even apologized for the inconvenience of having to bring her here.

"We just need to ask a few questions, if you would please come with us," Captain Grusow said in surprisingly good German.

Zara nodded and followed them. It didn't matter whether she agreed or not, they'd ask her their questions anyway. She relaxed slightly when they led her upstairs and through the menacing metal doors that kept the U-Boot sealed from the rest of the building and the world.

Up here it was surprisingly dark, since the sunlight streaming through the windows was no match for the merciless light bulb hammering down in her cell.

"Please sit. Would you like some water?"

"Yes." Her tongue stuck to the roof of her mouth and she yearned to quench her thirst.

Captain Grusow snapped his fingers and moments later a

woman who looked like one of the cleaning ladies Zara had seen earlier brought her a glass of water.

"Thanks," Zara said, but the woman didn't even look up, and instead hurried away backwards until she reached the door and disappeared through it.

The first questions were innocent enough, and Zara's nerves slowly relaxed as she provided information about her name, date and location of birth, address and occupation.

"What's your father's name?"

"Karl Theodor Ulbert."

"SS-Obersturmführer Ulbert?"

Zara saw Captain Grusow's lip twitch and a sinking feeling overwhelmed her. "Yes." Her voice came out weak.

Grusow smiled. "Your father was responsible for the setup of several concentration camps and then became Kommandant in Mauthausen, is this right?"

She was too panic-stricken to utter a word.

"Is this right?" Grusow asked again, this time with a noticeable impatient streak in his voice.

"Yes, this is right."

The captain nodded, seemingly content. His next question caught her off guard. "So, what did you do?"

"Me? What do you mean?"

"Did you help the innocent people in the camp?"

"People in the camp?" Zara repeated his question like a nitwit. Then it dawned on her. He was accusing her of being an accomplice. She looked up and realized Captain Grusow was waiting for an answer. The stretching silence between them became unnerving and she hastily said, "I was... I was only sixteen. My mother kept me at home."

"You're refusing to take responsibility for your actions?"

"I didn't do anything. I never even entered the camp, except for one occasion where I ran off, because I was so shocked."

"You admit that you were shocked by the things happening

and still didn't see fit to take action? To rescue those innocent people? Do you know that with your inaction you actually murdered these people?"

"They were enemies of the Reich..." she said, repeating the lame excuse her father had given her and that she'd used to silence her qualms so often until she'd actually believed it to be true.

"Women and children?" He gave her a reptilian grin, seemingly basking in his ability to corner her.

"I was only a child myself. I didn't do anything."

"That's what everyone says. Nobody had any responsibility, just like nobody was a Nazi. I want to know: how could an entire nation of non-Nazis follow this madman Hitler?"

Zara furrowed her brows. He wasn't actually expecting her to have an answer for this, was he? Like anyone in Germany she'd gone through the denazification process and had filled out dozens of sheets disclosing everything even remotely connected to working for the Nazis. Member of the *Bund Deutscher Mädel*. Volunteer for the *Winterhilfswerk*, a charity collecting donations for the less fortunate Germans, especially during the inclement months. "I was exonerated by the Americans. Category V."

"Well, we're not the Americans." He shook his head with a sad expression.

That much she'd already noticed. There was a reason why she'd wanted to leave Berlin and start working as a housemaid with an American family in Wiesbaden, far away from the Soviet sphere of influence, where people were habitually kidnapped and brought to secret prisons like this one or shipped straight away to a gulag in Siberia.

"Where is your father?" The question snapped through the room like the crack of a whip. The sinking feeling turned into full-blown panic as the realization set in. They were after her father, and she was simply a means to an end. If she couldn't deliver her father – and she had no idea where he was – she wouldn't be of any further use to them and they might simply dispose of her.

"I have no idea. He disappeared right before the end of the war, leaving my mother and me to fend for ourselves."

Grusow's fist slammed down on the table and she jumped. "And you want me to believe this?"

"It's the truth. Please, I'm not lying to you. I told this to the Americans when they conquered Linz and I told it again to your people when I arrived in Berlin."

"That was three years ago."

"Nothing has changed. My father never tried to contact me. And even if he appeared, I would want nothing to do with him!"

His brow twitched. "Look, this is where I don't believe you. You were his favorite child, and you're trying to make me believe he never contacted you?"

Zara flinched. For strangers it might seem that way, because her father had always indulged and pampered her. Showed her off. The good German girl who could cook so well and would soon bear many children for the Führer. A shiver raced down her spine. At fifteen she'd been promised in marriage – without even being asked – to a friend of her father's at least double her age, and only his premature death on the battlefield had saved her from that fate.

Her father had always preferred her two brothers, because she was just a girl. He had never even considered her an actual person, more like a prized possession, a piece of jewelry that was nice to look at and caused admiration all around. But she wouldn't tell any of this to Captain Grusow.

"He never contacted me. He escaped just in time before the Americans liberated Mauthausen and I haven't seen or heard from him since."

"Do you know where he is?"

Zara had an inkling where he could be. In certain circles the existence of rat lines was an open secret, and everyone knew Argentina was the favorite destination of high-ranking Nazis. "He could be anywhere. And since both the Soviets and the Americans are still after him, I doubt he'll ever return to Germany."

"That's where you're wrong," Captain Grusow said after a long silence. "Your father must return, because his money is running out. We know he's been a key person in hiding valuable artifacts that belong to the Soviet Union. Sooner rather than later he will surface and try to sell them."

"What? That's ridiculous." Zara's eyes became wide with shock. Her father had never been the type to appreciate the fine arts, since he was more drawn to everything motorized. Expensive cars, elegant planes, powerful tanks. Anything that had a motor fascinated him, but try as she might, she couldn't imagine him admiring a classic painting.

Captain Grusow leaned back in his chair, training his eyes on her. She couldn't decipher whether he believed her or not and decided to wait for his next move, when someone slapped her from behind. The impact came so unexpectedly that she would have fallen from her chair, if the same person who slapped her hadn't simultaneously grabbed her arm to hold her in place.

Zara rubbed her burning cheek with her free hand. The taste of blood on her tongue brought back disturbing memories of what other Soviet soldiers had done to her shortly after her so-called liberation, and her brain refused to work any longer.

Much later she woke on the cold and damp concrete floor in her windowless cell, every single bone in her body aching. She forced herself up on all fours and crawled to the wooden cot in the corner. Struggling to get onto it, she finally rolled into a ball and blissfully passed out again.

6

GLENN

With a horrible headache, Glenn dressed and followed the other soldiers to the canteen. Last night had been wild. After one too many drinks in the Café de Paris, he'd had a quick shag in the bushes, before he'd somehow stumbled back to the barracks.

After downing huge quantities of coffee and equally huge amounts of donuts, the hammering in his head slowly became bearable. Looking up, he recognized one of the guys he'd played basketball with the day before.

"Hey, Glenn, what are you up to?" Ryan asked.

"Nothing much."

"You up for teaching basketball to some kids?"

"Not really, I'd rather nurse my hangover and sleep all day." Under normal circumstances Glenn never refused an opportunity to play his favorite game, and teaching kids was something he enjoyed immensely. But his head was killing him.

"Come on. The kids are great. You'll have plenty of fun, and you'll be doing your country a service," Ryan pleaded with him.

"Because I'm teaching some spoiled army brats how to snag a basket?" Glenn chuckled.

"On the contrary. This is part of the re-education program for German kids. We have established a Youth House in each of the boroughs in our sector where they can hang out and meet, or participate in our athletics program. We're teaching them team spirit and democracy through playing basketball, baseball or football with our troops."

Glenn didn't have the slightest idea such a program existed. Another disadvantage of being stuck in the idyllic, yet utterly boring, Bavarian countryside. "Well, then, I guess I can't refuse."

"I'll meet you at two p.m. at the entrance gate, then?" Ryan asked.

"Sure, if you find me an aspirin first."

Ryan directed him to the medical station and half an hour later, Glenn was lying on his bunk again, getting some much needed shuteye. After lunch he met up with Ryan to walk over to the Youth House about five hundred yards further down the street.

"Most of the kids don't speak English," Ryan warned him.

Despite the language problems Glenn communicated well with his team, talking with hands and feet, and how much was there to say during a competitive game, anyway?

In the end, Glenn's team won against Ryan's and the kids stormed him with questions about daily life in America. With the help of a translator he answered any and all questions, save those about politics, because that was strictly off-limits.

One of the youths, a twelve-year-old boy called Hans came up to him and Glenn said, "You have good hand-eye coordination."

Hans' face brightened. "Thank you. I come here every week since they started the Youth House. This is the one thing I look forward to."

"You do?" Glenn didn't know what to say, but sensed that the boy needed to talk.

"Yes. Living in Berlin is so dull. I mean, there's nothing to do, except scrounge the ruins for shrapnel. Not that there's much left, and the adults chase us away anyway. But here, here we can just be and have fun. I like to play basketball."

"Why don't you play it at home with your friends, too?"

Hans stared at Glenn as if he were dumb. "We don't have a ball."

Glenn wanted to say something but closed his mouth and rubbed his chin. These kids weren't spoiled army brats like Charles' kids John and Lisa. Hans' mother probably had to spend the little money she earned on food and housing, with nothing left for luxuries like a basketball or proper shoes for her son.

He instantly felt bad and decided to ask Ryan whether it was possibly to buy a ball somewhere and give one to Hans.

"Davidson!" a voice called and he turned his head to see General Harris entering the Youth Club. "What the hell are you doing here, Davidson?" Harris bristled before Glenn even had the opportunity to greet him.

"Sir, I was asked to help out with the basketball training. This is a great program you have going here."

Harris looked slightly mollified but immediately his stare darkened again, "Who allowed you to leave the garrison?"

"Sir? I didn't know I needed to ask for permission."

"You are under security arrest!"

Glenn faltered. This could only be a misunderstanding because he wasn't aware of having done anything wrong. At least nothing that warranted such a severe punishment. "May I ask what I have done?"

Harris looked perplexed for a moment. "Hasn't anyone told you?"

"No."

"Well, then you'll find out soon enough. For now, you'll have to return to the garrison with me." Harris turned to walk away and Glenn hurried to keep up with him. "It's not your fault, but we can't have you walking around Berlin. You have to stay at the headquarters until further notice."

Glenn nodded, not daring to ask why or what. It might have something to do with the cloak-and-dagger operation flying liquor to Berlin, but none of it made any sense.

On their short walk back to headquarters Harris' mood seemed to brighten and he asked, "What do you think about our athletics program?"

"It was the first time I heard of it today and I was quite skeptical, but after seeing the kids I think it's a magnificent program."

Harris nodded. "The Russians are convinced we're using it as a front to indoctrinate the German youth with our political beliefs."

"They do?" Glenn paused for a moment, running a hand through his damp hair. "That's ridiculous. There's nothing less political than a good game."

"Exactly my words." Harris looked at him with a slight smile. "You may not know this, because you're not based in Berlin, but my Soviet counterpart General Sokolov has accused me of every crime under the sun for trying to give these kids a happy time once in a while. I have two teenage sons myself and I know exactly how these kids learn best about moral values. Definitely not by forcing them to attend some communist youth organization."

"Yes, sir."

"And our soldiers love it as well, because they can show off their skills at the game and have fun teaching the kids. It's good for both sides."

They reached the garrison and Harris dismissed Glenn with the assurance that his confinement wouldn't last long. With nothing else to do and no way to go out on the town that night, he took a shower and then flopped down on the bed, reading all the Berlin newspapers he could get his hands on.

Two days later Glenn was ordered into General Harris' office, where the general handed him a newspaper with the headline *New Deutsche Mark introduced in the Western zones.*

"Can you guess what was in the crates?"

Glenn squinted his eyes. No...that wasn't possible. He'd transported millions of Deutsche Mark to the capital without having the slightest inkling. "Money?"

"Our Plan B, to be precise. If the Soviets retaliate and include Berlin in their currency reform, which I fully expect, we are prepared."

Although the actual operation preparing the currency reform had been top secret, everyone had seen it coming. The Western allies had meticulously excluded the capital from the scope of their currency reform – mostly to avoid another clash with their Soviet partners.

"Wouldn't that be a violation of the quadripartite rule?" Glenn asked.

Harris gave a wry cough. "That shows you haven't been in Berlin for long. Those cutthroat liars and thieves care about the quadripartite agreement only when it serves them. But I'm done with their antics."

"May I ask a question?"

"Go ahead."

"Why me and why didn't you just tell me?"

Harris laughed. "One of the briefed pilots fell ill and we needed a quick replacement. It had to be someone not from Wiesbaden or Frankfurt, and Colonel Gardner recommended you. By the way, you're scheduled to return to Oberpfaffen-hofen this afternoon."

Glenn made a mental note to thank Charles for the unex-pected trip to Berlin, but would also give him a piece of his mind for not forewarning him. "One more thing. How much money was in that aircraft?"

"I have ordered two hundred fifty million Deutsche Mark to be marked with the letter B and flown into Berlin."

Glenn's jaw dropped to the floor. "That's a helluva lot."

"Eleven planeloads, ten tons each, to be exact."

7

VLADI

R ed Army Intelligence Captain Vladimir Rublev was having tea. Since the British had introduced the habit of afternoon tea to Berlin, he'd adopted this tradition, changing just one small detail: he always laced his tea heavily with vodka, the Russian national drink.

Sitting at the window and looking into the lush gardens of the Soviet Military Administration Headquarters in Karlshorst he mused about the next steps in the big plan to squeeze the Western Allies out of Berlin.

General Sokolov, the Soviet Kommandant in Berlin and counterpart to *The Beast of Berlin*, as the American Kommandant General Harris was commonly known, had made a brilliant move the past week and walked out of the Kommandatura, while putting all the blame on the aforementioned beast.

Quadripartite rule over the German capital had effectively ceased, and the Soviet rulers could now implement phase two of the operation to run the other Allies out of Berlin.

Just what exactly they had planned, Vladi wasn't privy to and it rankled him to a great extent. They might plan a sudden coup, orchestrating loyal communists to overtake the German self-government bodies, supported by the threat of Soviet troops amassing at the city borders. Or they might continue where they stopped with the traffic controls in April, but this time in earnest.

His musings were cut short by an aide approaching him. "Comrade Captain, Lieutenant Colonel Propov is requiring you urgently."

Vladi suppressed a groan and downed the rest of his tea. "I'll be right there."

With long strides he walked upstairs to where the office of his direct boss lay, while wondering what exactly could be the reason for this summons. Urgent requests were never a good thing.

The door to Propov's office stood open and Vladi heard his heavy footfalls pacing the room, before he saw him. The situation must be dire. Propov stopped the moment Vladi entered and said, "I see you still prefer that shabby look over your uniform."

As usual, Vladi had chosen to wear black pants, a simple dark blue shirt and a black leather jacket, which he felt suited him better in his line of work. It wasn't necessary to be recognized as a member of the Red Army when on a surveillance mission or stirring up trouble with the Americans.

While his bosses mocked the attire, they had never ordered him not to wear it. They could see the benefits. But appearances had to be kept up, and a denigrating remark by a superior was expected. Such were the rules.

"Comrade Propov. You wanted to see me."

Propov paused for a moment as if trying to remember the reason for his request, and then began shouting, "This is unacceptable. Utterly unacceptable! Those wicked thugs think they can just do whatever they want!"

Vladi barely suppressed a sigh of relief. Propov was ranting about the Americans again, for which topic he was very grateful, since an unequivocal damnation of every single one of their actions, independently of their nature, was always appropriate. "Absolutely, Comrade Propov. It is an outrageous thing to do!"

Propov squinted his eyes at Vladi and hissed, "And it's all your fault!"

My fault? What can I possibly have done to encourage the Americans in whatever shenanigans they have committed now? He bowed his head. "I am afraid I don't follow you."

"Obersturmführer Ulbert has surfaced."

Vladi's eyes almost popped out of his head. Obersturmführer Ulbert had been missing since the end of the war, presumably in Argentina, and half of the world was after him. He had not only been the Kommandant of the Mauthausen concentration camp, but also one of the masterminds behind the extermination concept. If the Americans had found him first, that was a major publicity disaster and Propov would need a scapegoat — Vladi.

"When and where?" Vladi stammered.

"It would have been your job to know this, now wouldn't it?" The verdict was clear, and Vladi's days in Red Army Intelligence were numbered. It didn't matter that he'd been busy carrying out General Sokolov's orders, harassing American passengers on the trains to the Western zones, therefore he preferred not to defend himself. He waited for the inevitable punishment, while Propov grew even more agitated and shouted, "Due to your utter incompetence, the NKVD questioned her, and not we. Do you know how dumb Captain Grusow makes me look?"

Goosebumps broke out on Vladi's arms. NKVD officer Captain Grusow was Propov's personal nemesis, because Grusow and his men had the annoying habit of overstepping their authority and interfering with Red Army Intelligence affairs. Vladi really was in serious trouble.

. . .

"THEY PICKED her up trying to flee to the American zone. Why didn't we get her? We are controlling the trains! Where were you and why didn't you arrest her first?"

"Her? Pardon my ignorance, Comrade Propov, weren't we talking about SS-Obersturmführer Ulbert?"

"The daughter!"

Which daughter? Despite not having the slightest idea what Propov was talking about, Vladi kept his mouth shut. Years of formal education in the Soviet school system, in the Komsomol and in the Red Army had ingrained upon him that questions were to be avoided at all costs.

Even when one was encouraged to ask, it was better to formulate only the kind of questions that were guaranteed not to be controversial. Hence, he decided to go with the flow and later find out the details of said daughter.

Why hadn't he been alerted that she was trying to flee to the American zone, undoubtedly to meet up with her father?

"I agree. The NKVD overstepped their authority once again. What do you want me to do? Write a formal complaint?" The NKVD and Red Army Intelligence had competed with each other for as long as Vladi had been part of the organization, and often deliberately hindered the other organization's work – something Vladi suspected was intended by the higher-ups, so they would always have two irons in the fire on any operation.

Writing a complaint would serve for nothing, but it would document their discontent and might be useful later on for blaming the NKVD if something went wrong. Cover your ass – that was the first strategy anyone in the Soviet Union learned.

Propov waved his hand. "No need. After three days of interrogation they couldn't get anything useful out of her, announced she knew nothing and will let her go."

Vladi's gut twisted. He had no qualms getting into a bloody

fight, harassing someone or resorting to a bit of *physical intimidation* as he liked to call it. That was just part of the business, but he drew the line at beating up or otherwise torturing a woman. That was something only the NKVD thugs engaged in.

"All the better for us, because it just shows how inept they are, arresting the wrong person."

Propov shook his head. "On the contrary, it shows that they're rookies at interrogation techniques, and that's our opportunity to show those rotten bastards how it's done professionally. You will arrest her again and get the information we need."

Vladi swayed for a moment, before he looked firmly at his superior's face. "Certainly, Comrade Propov. I'll arrest her again. What exactly do you want me to get from her?"

"Her father."

"And...if she doesn't know where he is?"

"She does. Ensure she'll tell you."

The blood drained from Vladi's face. He dreaded the prospect of having to torture a woman. More so, because he was convinced she didn't possess the information everyone was after. Nobody withstood three days of NKVD treatment without spilling the beans.

"My secretary will brief you on the details. If her father is in Germany, I want to be the one to arrest him."

Vladi left the room, cursing his bad luck for getting yet another assignment he didn't want to have. Why couldn't his superiors solve their feud without involving him in this? Now he would have to talk to the detested Captain Grusow, strongarm him into sharing all the information the NKVD possessed — and capture the poor woman again.

Propov's secretary briefed him on the whereabouts of Zara Ulbert and gave him a picture of her. When he looked at it, he all but toppled over. He knew this beautiful woman who resembled Snow White with her ebony hair, cherry-red lips and buttermilk skin.

He'd seen her several times at the Café de Paris. She was friends with the glamorous singer Brunhilde von Sinnen. That might complicate his endeavor, because Bruni had been the official mistress of General Harris until his wife arrived in Berlin not long ago. Tempted to scream out his frustration, he gritted his teeth, took the photograph and left the Soviet Military Administration headquarters to find Zara Ulbert and squeeze the secret of her father's location from her.

He had to be extra careful though, because if her friend Bruni alerted the Americans that would only cause the kind of trouble General Sokolov hated. For the devil's sake, why couldn't the clueless NKVD louts keep their hands still and why was it always him who had to face the music?

8

ZARA

Zara was rolled into a ball on the wooden cot, every bone, muscle and cell in her body aching. She had stopped counting the amount of beatings she'd received and with the few brain cells still working properly she wondered why she was even alive and what the Soviets would do to her next. She was exhausted to the core and wished nothing more than to sleep, but the drumming pain in her freezing body combined with the merciless neon light hammering down on her prevented the blissful state of sliding into dreamland.

Whenever she'd finally fall asleep, miraculously the door opened and she was rudely awakened by dreadful shaking or an equally dreadfully bucket of cold water poured over her head. At times she wondered whether a few precious minutes of sleep were worth the brutal rousing, or whether it was preferable to try and stay awake.

But for the past – how many? – days she'd been left alone in her misery. Twice a day someone came to bring her food and disappeared without a word. Her distraught mind began seeing things that weren't there and right now she saw the door to her cell open and a strange woman enter her cell, carrying something. Zara instinctively shrunk back on her cot, trying to become one with the wall behind her in the futile hope the woman wouldn't notice her.

"Don't be afraid," the woman said and took a cloth from the bowl filled with water. Zara had difficulties focusing on the woman's actions, but soon realized that she was cleaning Zara's wounds.

Zara was too apathetic to flinch at the stabs of pain searing through her body when the wet cloth touched her skin. After the woman had washed Zara and combed her hair, she said, "Get up, you're being released."

It took Zara a few seconds to comprehend the meaning of the words, but then she got up, suppressing a pained groan. One million questions pooled at the tip of her tongue, but she bit her lip, fearing a single wrong word might make her captors change their minds.

As she walked up the staircase from the basement to the dreadful metal doors, her steps became springy despite the dull aches in her body. Just the prospect of being free again made her forget the physical pain.

In front of the building the same dark gray vehicle she had arrived in was waiting, and for a moment her heart stopped beating. But instead of being rudely shoved into the backseat, the driver got out to open the passenger door for her.

"Train station," he said and then fell into a silence for the rest of the trip. She recognized the route they were taking from Hohenschönhausen in the direction of the city center until they arrived at the Ostbahnhof, the train station in the Soviet sector. Her breath caught in her lungs and she would have bolted from the vehicle, if it weren't for the dozens of Soviet soldiers milling about in the vicinity of the train station.

Her release must have been a ruse and she was destined to be sent east, to Siberia or some other inhabitable place, because why else would they drive her to this train station and not the ones in the Western sectors?

"Borders closed," the driver said in his bad German.

She wanted to ask him what that meant, but her sleep-deprived brain couldn't come up with the Russian phrase and his German apparently was exhausted with those two words. He waved at a soldier and after a rapid-fire conversation, where the only word she understood was Marienborn, he looked at her. "You go."

The other soldier took over, organized a ticket for her to Marienborn, the town at the inner-German border, and then put her onto the train. Miraculously her suitcase was already in the compartment, looking undamaged and as if it had been waiting for her all these days, wondering why she was delayed. She flopped onto the seat and let out a deep sigh when the Soviet soldier vanished.

Her entire life had been turned upside down these past days, but she was determined not to give up. As soon as she crossed the border into the British zone, she would never look back or set a single foot into the Soviet zone again.

The man sitting opposite her, who was dressed in a smart business suit, was reading an issue of the newspaper *Neues Deutschland*, the communist SED party organ. She leaned forward to decipher the headline. *Call of the Soviet Military Administration.*

What heinous thing did they want to call attention to now? Usually she didn't read this communist propaganda newspaper, but since she'd been literally swept from the face of the earth, for God only knew how long, she read on:

The American, British and French military authorities have illegally carried out a separate currency reform in Germany's western occupation zones. As a result, the population of the Soviet zone and Berlin was exposed to the serious danger that both the Soviet occupation zone of Germany and the Greater Berlin area would be flooded with canceled money and that economic life would be completely disorganized.

A currency reform? When had that happened? Her gaze fell onto the date, and she rubbed her eyes in shock.

"Excuse me, is this newspaper from today?" she asked.

He looked up at her with the indulgence many men showed when talking to a young woman they considered stupid. "Naturally. Nothing is older than yesterday's news."

Zara glued her gaze to the grayish paper in his hands, willing the numbers of the date to change in front of her eyes. But as much as she tried, there was no doubt. Today was June 25, 1948. Her world seemed to crumble to pieces and she felt as if someone had catapulted her straight into the future.

She had spent close to three weeks in the U-Boot at Hohenschönhausen prison. With that realization, fear seeped into her bones; her employers must be livid and might not want her to work for them anymore. Perhaps, they'd already found a new maid. She might as well stay in Berlin for the time being. But before she could jump off the train, the locomotive whistled and set into motion.

About an hour into the journey, the train stopped in between stations. Cold fear grabbed at Zara's heart as she experienced déjà vu. Loud Russian voices and heavy footfalls approached the compartment. Her fingers folded around the train ticket and travel permission she had been given.

The door opened and a rather handsome young man in his late twenties with short blond hair peeked inside. Relief flooded her system when she realized he didn't wear the loathsome Soviet Army uniform, but black pants and a black leather jacket. She scolded herself for seeing ghosts and looked at him in a friendlier manner. He returned the smile and moments later she noticed how recognition hit him and his grin broadened.

"Zara Ulbert. So glad I found you! Would you please come

with me?" His deep voice was pleasant and his German flaw-
less, but with a distinct pronunciation to it that she couldn't
quite place.

She squinted her eyes, trying to figure out how he knew her,
but came up blank. "Excuse me, should I know you?"

The businessman sitting opposite her peeked around from
behind his newspaper, intent on not drawing attention to
himself, while the blond man bent down to Zara in a very intimate manner. His breath brushed her cheek as he whispered
into her ear, "I'll introduce myself later. For now, you can follow
me without making a scene or I can get the military police to
drag you out of this train. What will it be?"

Despite the softly whispered words she heard the threat
loud and clear and wondered what kind of guy he was. He
looked like a black marketeer or a common smalltime criminal,
but then he most certainly wouldn't threaten her with the
police. Looking at his steel blue eyes from nearby, her brain
clicked and she connected his looks with the barely noticeable
accent and immediately knew where she'd seen him before. He
was one of the regulars at the Café de Paris where Bruni
worked. A Russian. He always wore the same black leather
jacket and nobody seemed to know exactly what he did for the
Soviet Administration.

Zara's eyes darted around the compartment and fell on the
businessman sitting opposite her, who'd shriveled, using his
newspaper like a shield and pretending not to notice anything
out of the normal. She couldn't count on his help, nor could she
dash for the window and jump, because she glimpsed at least
three Soviet soldiers loitering outside, smoking cigarettes.

"How could I spurn such a gracious invitation?" she asked,
mustering all the courage she could.

"Good choice." He seemed sincerely pleased and cast his
eyes upward, asking with a nod. "Is this your suitcase?"

"Yes."

She was about to get up and reach for the handle, but he preempted her and pulled the valise from the overhead rack with an ease that made her hiss in a breath. He was about her own height and his blue eyes leveled with hers as he had the chutzpah to offer his arm. "Shall we?"

Zara was rendered speechless by his cocky attitude, but took his arm as gracefully as possible and walked with him from the train. He jumped onto the gravel and then held out his hand to help her down. She glowered at him and wanted to refuse his help, but the throbbing in her thigh changed her opinion.

On the other side of the rampart waited another gray military vehicle for them and her knees began to wobble. He must have noticed her distress, because he grabbed her elbow tighter. Once he'd helped her into the passenger seat, he took off his leather jacket, threw it onto the backseat and positioned himself behind the wheel.

"Pleased to meet you," he said, holding out his hand to shake hers.

She chose to ignore the hand and demanded to know, "Who are you and what is this all about?"

"Forgive my manners. I'm Captain Vladimir Rublev, Red Army Intelligence."

All blood drained from her head and her eyes frantically darted around, judging the speed of the vehicle and calculating whether it was viable to jump out. But before she'd even finished the thought, she felt his hand on her arm – neither rough nor hurtful, but strangely reassuring.

"That's a really bad idea. I'm not here to hurt you. I just have a few questions for you."

Zara didn't believe a single word, since all of this was part of their tactic: feigning kindness and then resorting to physical pain if the victim didn't tell them what they wanted to know. "I already told your colleagues that I don't know where my father is."

"The brutish Captain Grusow isn't actually a colleague and I'm so very sorry for the inconvenience his men caused." He made a pregnant pause, before he took his eyes off the road and peered at her intensely. "I'm not entirely convinced you told them everything."

His words punched her in the gut, as forceful as the physical blows the men in Hohenschönhausen had dealt her.

"You think you can torture me better than they did?"

With his gaze darting between her and the road ahead, she imagined seeing an appreciative smirk on his face. "Our department are not barbarians. In fact, I had hoped you would be open to reason and we could have a conversation between adults, where I ask you some simple questions and you answer them."

The proposal sounded reassuring, but she wouldn't let his incredibly charming manner lull her into believing a single word he said. As far as she was concerned every Russian was a cutthroat criminal and soulless monster.

The car stopped. "We have arrived."

Zara stepped from the car and looked around. She'd been too busy keeping her fear in check to pay attention to the route they'd been taking and had no idea where they were. But it wasn't Hohenschönhausen, or anything prisonlike. She stared incredulously at the lovely two-story redbrick building in front of her and the vast gardens with an old stock of trees surrounding it. She vaguely remembered an open iron gate they'd passed a few minutes back and assumed it had been closed the moment they drove through, heavily guarded along with the perimeter of this grand estate.

"Where are we?" she asked.

"I'll have to kill you if I tell you."

Zara jumped backwards, crashing into the open passenger door and stumbling when it closed with a smashing sound.

"I was joking," he said, looking rather contrite.

He wasn't as slick as the other men who'd interrogated her and despite his thuggish appearance, he seemed to be honest. She couldn't explain it, but something about him reassured her and she brought up the courage to say, "That was a rather bad joke, because your colleagues from the NKVD were very close to doing just that."

"They're not my colleagues." He appeared honestly offended, gritting his teeth before continuing. "I already told you that our department are not barbarians. But I must apologize, it was an inappropriate joke in this situation."

He led the way to the house and opened the unlocked door. So far Zara hadn't noticed any human being, save for the two of them. She gazed at his broad shoulders and the muscled arms and didn't delude herself into believing she could be a match for him.

Whatever he had in store for her, he didn't need armed guards to help him get what he wanted. Goosebumps rose on her arms despite the warm June temperatures. So far, Captain Rublev had behaved like a gentleman, but she would bet her last *Pfennig* that he could behave more in accordance with his thuggish appearance.

They entered a room furnished with an antique desk made of dark wood, and two chairs of the same style, one to either side. The entire building reeked of distinguished elegance and she wondered to whom it might have belonged before the Soviets requisitioned it. Probably some Nazi official, who in turn had stolen it from a Jew.

"Would you like something to drink?" Captain Rublev asked.

She squinted her eyes suspiciously at him, but decided to take him up on the offer. "Yes, please."

He got up and opened the door, turning around, looking at her with that devastating grin. Under different circumstances she might have been attracted to him. But he was her kidnapper and a member of the loathed oppressing power. "Don't disappear, please."

Zara almost had to laugh at his antics, since she doubted they were alone here. Just because she hadn't seen anyone didn't mean there weren't any people around. The perimeter of the house surely was heavily guarded and the soldiers – or dogs – would catch her within minutes. Still, she couldn't resist countering his cheeky remark. "What happens if I try?"

He smirked and moved his flat hand across his throat. He made it seem like a joke, but she knew he was deadly serious. If she ran he would kill her. What a reassuring prospect!

Zara settled on one of the chairs, studying the delicate wooden carvings on the wall panels until he returned with two full water glasses. He put one in front of her and drank half of his glass with one gulp.

She picked up her glass and took a generous sip. Then she gasped. A fire-like sensation burned down her throat and the fear that he'd poisoned her trickled into her stomach, countering the heat with an icy chill.

Still gasping for breath, she asked, "What the hell is this?"

"Vodka."

"Vodka?"

"Yes, don't you like it?"

"You offered me something to drink!"

"And? What's wrong with vodka? It's completely drinkable. See?" He picked up his glass and emptied it.

Despite the circumstances, Zara started laughing. "I guess you're right. Nothing wrong with downing a water glass full of vodka when you've been through hell, and just when you thought Hades spit you back out to return to earth, you're kidnapped by someone else."

He squinted his eyes. "Who is Hades? You said the NKVD kidnapped you..."

"You're right, I need vodka for this." Zara took up her glass and downed it in a single gulp, not caring what the alcohol did to her stomach or her brain. She'd never tolerated more alcohol than a glass of wine and knew this amount of liquor would knock her out before long, but for all she was concerned, being too drunk to remember a thing of what might happen next was the preferable condition to be in. To hell with the consequences.

9

VLADI

Vladi stared incredulously at the woman sitting in front of him. *I shouldn't have given her the vodka.* He'd wanted her to feel at ease with him, to be less guarded, more talkative, but his plan had completely gone awry, because she'd decided to openly defy him.

"Where is your father?" he tried once more.

"I have already told you one thousand times. I don't know." Her beautiful brown eyes glowered at him, even as her voice rose to a scream. He wasn't afraid that someone would hear her, because if the guards did they'd only assume he was torturing her, but he needed her to cooperate. She wouldn't tell him anything the NKVD didn't already know if she didn't trust him.

"You insist that he hasn't contacted you?" Vladi ran a hand through his cropped hair. Usually women fell for his bad-boy charm and toppled over themselves to please him. But not her. It was annoying, to say the least.

She gave a dramatic sigh. "How often do I have to say this to get it into your brains? He hasn't contacted me. And if you would have taken the time to read the protocols your colleagues—"

He cracked and yelled, "They aren't my colleagues!"

That insufferable woman waved her hand at him. "They are Russians, like you. They work for the same government. As far as I'm concerned they are your colleagues."

If she compared him to those brutes once more, he'd show her exactly how these deplorables would treat her. Irascibility was creeping up his spine like a tiger ready to attack if this woman uttered one more defiant word. It would be such a fantastic release to wrap his big hands around her slender neck, squeezing until she begged for her life.

Then she'd finally behave reasonably and do what was good for her. Instead of calming her down, the vodka had raised her spirits to the point where she derived pleasure from defying him.

Apparently impatient with his lack of response to her last remark, she jumped up and pushed her finger into his chest. "Criminal thugs. Bastards and louts. All of you."

Enraged, he jumped up, digging his fingers into the flesh of her shoulders. He so wished he could scowl down on her, but since she was exceptionally tall for a woman, his eyes were level with hers and the crazy glint in them made him reconsider his approach.

He would not be able to break her. Captain Grusow had tried and hadn't gotten any useful information. Strangling her and making her beg for her life was a nice vision and he was more than tempted to give in to his desire, especially since nobody would hold him accountable. But reason won out. He had a mission to accomplish and information to tease from her. And he had a soft spot for beautiful women, all the more if they looked sweet and innocent like this one.

The violent image of his hands around her neck was replaced by a more pleasurable one of her naked body beneath him, writhing and whimpering. Arousal surged in his loins, shoving his violent irascibility aside. He removed the fingers from her shoulders, noticing the glint of pain when the blood returned to her flesh.

"I'm sorry," he said, looking straight into her eyes. "I tend to get very upset when someone insults me."

Her eyes widened, and he could read a multitude of emotions in them. Shock, relief, disbelief, wariness, and gratitude.

This gave him an idea. "I believe you."

"Oh, suddenly you do?" The sarcasm was dripping from her voice and again his fingers itched to squeeze her throat until she shut up. Why did this woman have to be so incredibly annoying?

"I have two options," he stared at her, warning her not to contradict him, because his patience was hanging on a very thin thread. "Since you seem to have no information, I could either send you to a gulag in Siberia or you could work for us."

"I'd rather die in Siberia than sell my soul to the devil," she spat at him.

"Look, some unfortunate mistakes have been made, but that doesn't mean all Soviets are bad people." Vladi could barely keep his voice even.

"Oh, so torturing me has been an unfortunate mistake? Do you even listen to yourself? All I ever wanted was to live in peace. I had so hoped for this to happen when the war finally ended, but then your soldiers made my life a living hell, and when I finally got the chance to leave Berlin behind, your people arrested me and threw me into their dungeon."

Vladi felt his ears burning. What his compatriots had done to Zara wasn't right; he certainly didn't condone the raping nor the torturing of women. But it wasn't his fault and there was nothing he could do about it. Criticizing the government was a surefire way to end up in the exactly same place he'd threatened to send Zara.

"And now you have the guts to ask me to work for the very

people who ordered all this? How can you be so...so...so vile?" Visibly exhausted by her tirade she took a clumsy step forward and collapsed directly into his arms.

He stared down at the slack body in his arms and wondered what he should do with her.

10

GLENN

"Have you heard?" Teddy, Glenn's friend and long-time co-pilot, came rushing into the break room.

"What now? A cow has mooed?" Glenn asked. Out here in Oberpfaffenhofen, the most excitement one could expect was a fight between two drunken farmers.

"There's a blockade going on and they are looking for pilots."

"Blockade? Pilots? What are you talking about?"

"The Berlin thing."

"And what does this have to do with us?"

"Are you deaf? Berlin has been blockaded by the Soviets. We're flying supplies into the city. For this, pilots are needed in Wiesbaden. Urgently. Preferably pilots with birds at their disposal. Just like us."

Glenn's curiosity was piqued and he looked up from the pool table, where he was about to knock in the last ball. "I still have no idea what you're talking about, but if it involves flying, I am game."

"At last someone with some sense." Teddy looked around the room, where most of the men were slouching. "The rest of you keep talking nonsense and boring yourselves to death, Glenn and I are off to Wiesbaden."

Glenn followed Teddy to the CO's office and asked, "Are you sure this is a thing?"

"Told you it is. A buddy just called me. They are desperate for more pilots."

"And you think the old man will agree to send us over there just like that?" Glenn had served long enough to know that nothing was ever done in a hurry in the military.

But he oughtn't to have worried. When they entered their CO's office, the sturdy man looked up from his desk even as he put down the phone receiver and gave them a once-over. "I take it you're here because of the Berlin thing?"

"Yes, sir," Glenn and Teddy said in unison.

"Alright. Pack all your stuff, hop onto one of the Skytrains and get your asses over there. Report to the flight office in Wiesbaden, they will give you your orders."

Glenn had never been as fast in and out of his CO's office. Usually the man liked to give a speech about regulations and precautions, but not this time. Twenty minutes later, Glenn and Teddy were fully packed, all of their belongings in kitbags slung over their respective shoulders.

As they approached the Skytrain they'd been assigned to take to Wiesbaden, they high-fived each other. "We are flying again, mate."

"Yes. We are."

AFTER AN UNEVENTFUL FLIGHT they stepped out of their plane at the Wiesbaden airbase, eager to load it up with cargo and continue on their next leg to Berlin. There, chaos abounded everywhere they looked and nothing was even remotely organized.

The rush of adrenaline tingled in Glenn's cells. This was it. The ultimate adventure akin to the good old days in the Wild West, where every man fended for himself. He looked at Teddy. "Well, seems we travelled faster than the news of our arrival."

"Let's find the flight office."

Glenn nodded, remembering where it was from his last time here, when he'd flown millions of Deutsche Mark to Berlin. A suspicion burgeoned. Was this blockade the retaliation General Harris had talked about? Was the vicious Soviet blockade a direct result of the currency reform?

He rubbed his chin, vowing to keep better tabs on politics, now that he was back in the thick of it, instead of hanging out between cows and sheep in the Alpine foothills.

They found the flight office and reported for duty, but the man behind the desk barely raised his bleary eyes from the lists in front of him. "Where did you come from?"

"Oberpfaffenhoffen."

"You have an aircraft at your disposal?"

"Yes. A Skytrain."

"Good." The officer's face took on a pleased expression. "At least your CO had the sense to send you over by plane. There's shiploads of pilots arriving here, but none of them bring a set of wings."

Glenn had already noticed dozens of men in uniform milling about the base. It truly was quite the mess.

"What are our orders?" Teddy asked.

"Orders?" The officer scoffed. "Get back to your craft before someone else takes it, find ground staff to fuel and load it up and off you go to Tempelhof Airport." He already waved them out his office, when he said almost as an afterthought, "You know the route, right?"

"Yes, sir. I flew to Tempelhof less than two weeks ago," Glenn answered.

The other man wiped beads of sweat from his forehead.

"Good. Very good. But now it's different. The Soviets may shoot you down if you leave the corridor. Understood?"

Glenn's adrenaline level spiked, pumping the blood in breakneck speed through his veins. Surely, the man was joking. The Soviets wouldn't shoot down their own allies, now would they?

Although, if they were capable of putting a siege on the German capital, they'd probably do anything. The knowledge added an extra layer of excitement.

"Strangest operation I've ever participated in," Teddy said as they were back on the airfield, searching for someone to fuel and load their Skytrain. Two hours later they boarded the cockpit, equipped with maps and the weather report, and started into the adventure called Operation Vittles.

"Aren't you excited to be flying again?" Glenn asked.

"Hell yes. And in Berlin we'll reward us with a nice German Fräulein." Teddy was already making plans to spend the night.

After an eventless flight, keeping strictly to the air corridor, they landed in Tempelhof Airport just before darkness settled over the country. Glenn loved flying into the sunset, when orange and red hues exploded in the sky, making it resemble a painter's canvas. Even though he wasn't usually the art-loving type, he could never get enough of looking at the constantly changing colors and patterns when the sun disappeared behind the horizon.

They disembarked the aircraft and reported to the flight office, where they were told they had to fly back in an hour, much to Teddy's disappointment. Nevertheless, they used the time to venture into the airport building to grab a bite. The room was full with crews coming from airbases all over the American zone in Germany, mostly Wiesbaden, Frankfurt/Main and Fritzlar.

"Great to be flying again, even if it's only a cargo machine, right?" Glenn said to a wiry man downing incredible amounts of coffee.

"I'd rather return stateside. This is folly," the other man answered, chewing on his sandwich.

"Come on, you can't be serious. What is better than flying?"

"What about a bed, regular meals, and a hot shower?" At Glenn's confused face the other man chuckled. "Is this your first day on the air bridge?"

"Yes, we just arrived in Wiesbaden from Ober'huffin'puffin." Teddy answered for Glenn.

"You ain't seen nothin' then. Good luck finding a bunk to hunker down when you're back." He turned around and went for another sandwich.

"What does he mean?" Glenn asked.

"You'll see soon enough. The entire organization is a complete mess," a very young crewman answered.

Glenn had gathered that much from his short stint hunting for fuel and cargo at the Wiesbaden airbase, but surely this wasn't the case with food and accommodations. This was the American Air Force after all, an exceptionally well-organized military organization that prided itself on discipline and order.

He didn't have time to pursue this thought, because a recently arrived crew came inside, storming the donut tray.

Munching, one of them said, "This is only a drop in the ocean, because how many supplies can we fly into the city per day? Three hundred tons? Maybe one thousand?"

"One thousand tons is a helluva lot," someone responded.

"Not when you consider there's two point two million people in the city. How much do you think they eat in a single day?"

Nobody knew, but everyone had an opinion and soon the room was full of wild guesses about the nutritional needs of a city the size of Berlin. In the end they agreed that one thousand tons was far too little, and three or four thousand tons was probably more like it.

"That's absolutely impossible," a guy called Jim said. "The cargo capacity of a Gooney Bird is three tons."

Glenn made a quick calculation in his head. "That's a minimum of one thousand aircraft landing and departing at Tempelhof every single day. Even if the airport operated twenty-four hours, which it doesn't, it would mean forty-two craft per hour or roughly one every 100 seconds."

"Impossible," Jim repeated his verdict.

"We don't even have that many Gooney Birds in all of Europe, let alone in Germany."

"And landing and starting at such small intervals wouldn't be safe."

"How can collisions be avoided if everyone is using the same corridor?"

Actually, there were three contractually agreed air corridors crossing the Soviet territory between Berlin and the Western zones, but only one of them to the American zone, while the two others lead into British territory.

"What about the Brits? Aren't they going to chip in?" Teddy asked.

"They are. I know for sure that they've been flying from Celle and Lübeck to Gatow, but they have maybe one tenth of the Gooneys that we have."

"And don't count on the French, since all the men and material they have are tied up in Indochina."

Glenn scratched his head. "The French don't even have an airbase in Berlin, and with just the two fields with those dilapidated landing strips we could have all the aircraft we wanted and still wouldn't be able to fly in the supplies needed."

Without their noticing, the airport commandant had entered the break room and interrupted the discussion, "We all know it's an impossible undertaking to supply a city this size by air. It's merely a symbolic act to show the Russians we are determined to fight them every step of the way. It'll buy us enough time to find a different solution. Whether it's diplomatic negotiations or our tanks rolling down the Autobahn." His emphasis made it clear which he preferred.

11

ZARA

Despite her blurred vision she realized that she wasn't in the same room anymore. Instead of the dark wood panels, the ceiling here was white and as her gaze travelled down the walls it stopped at the elegant castle-worthy light green arras with printed golden ornaments around white flowers.

Panicked, she tore her eyes completely open and found that she was lying in bed, covered by a thin linen sheet. She wiggled her bare feet and didn't dare to acknowledge how much of her clothes she was wearing beneath the linen sheet. She shot up in the bed, but a searing headache incapacitated her and she closed her eyes again, sinking back into the horizontal position.

The consequences of downing an entire water glass full of vodka attacked her with a vengeance and the urge to vomit joined the horrible headache. But since she hadn't eaten in such a long time, only bile came up and she cursed herself for being so stupid.

She had no memory about what had happened last night – it must have been last night, because the air streaming in through the tilted window had the fresh smell of early morning. Usually she liked the morning hours, when the world was so innocent and unspent, but today even the chirping of the birds caused vile hammering in her already hurting head.

Unable to keep a straight thought, she relaxed into her pillow, afraid to remember. Whatever had happened, it wouldn't hurt to ignore it. Moments later the door opened and Captain Rublev came inside with a full glass. "Are you feeling better?"

"No," she rasped.

His face took on a sorrowful expression. "I brought you something to drink."

"Vodka?"

"No, water."

She sat up to take the glass and flinched at the renewed waves of pain pulsating through her head. Her hands trembled and she spilled quite an amount, before she managed to get the liquid into her mouth. The cool freshness soaked up the awful aftertaste of alcohol mixed with bile and she swallowed it down, feeling how it ran down her throat.

"That bad?" he asked, honest concern etched into his face.

"I never drink more than a glass of wine, because I don't tolerate alcohol well," she managed to say.

"Yes, I already came to that conclusion when you collapsed on me last night."

Despite her pain, she felt her cheeks burn with embarrassment and instinctively pressed her legs together. God only knew what he'd made her do after she'd blacked out.

"Don't worry. Nothing bad happened." His lazy grin could mean anything, but she chose to ignore the nagging doubt in the back of her head and take his words at face value. Despite everything she actually started to like him. Another wave of nausea hit her and she swayed.

"That's a monster of a hangover you're nursing. Let me get something for you," he said, and disappeared.

Zara leaned against the wall, taking stock of the room. Apart from her bed, there was a wardrobe, a vanity table with a clouded mirror and a stool upholstered in the same material as the arras. With Captain Rublev gone, she gathered the courage to peek down her body and found that she was still wearing her dress and underthings. A heavy burden fell from her shoulders.

Moments later he returned with full hands. He sat the teacup on the vanity and held out a washcloth, saying, "Put this on your neck."

The cloth was hard and heavy, and it took her a moment to realize it was filled with ice cubes. When she positioned it on her neck, the icy cold took away her breath, but it didn't take long until the cold numbed the aches in her head and the nasty hammering was transformed into a dull pain.

"Better?"

"A lot."

"Drink this." He took the teacup and offered it to her.

The smell of chamomile wafted into her nostrils, immediately soothing her upset stomach as she sipped it in tiny slugs. When she was finished, she handed him the cup, searching for the right words. His eyes locked with hers and once again she was surprised at the kindness behind his rough appearance.

"Thank you," she said, wondering how they would continue from here. He was still her kidnapper and he still wanted to know where her father was. Vladi turned around, putting the teacup away, and she could sense he was stalling. When he finally looked at her again, she saw the determination in his eyes.

"I'll let you go."

"Let me go? Just like that?" She must be imagining things.

He shrugged. "Yes. It's clear that either you really don't know where your father is, or your resilience is much stronger than I'm prepared to break. Because contrary to your insults, I'm not a brute."

His words caused her to feel uncomfortable, but she buried the sensation of guilt beneath righteous indignation. "Are you expecting me to be grateful?"

His mouth spread into a lazy grin. "That would be nice for a change, but honestly I don't think you're capable of being nice."

Ouch. What an arrogant bastard. He was the one kidnapping and threatening her. So, who wasn't being nice? Although she had to admit he'd been as well-behaved as a Russian official could possibly be. She decided to make an effort and not antagonize him further. "Alright, I am grateful. Thank you so much for not being like your colleagues."

"They aren't my colleagues!" He went off like a Katyusha rocket launcher and she broke out in laughter.

He glared at her and for a moment she was afraid he'd harm her, but then his jaw relaxed and he announced, "We'll travel to Wiesbaden together tomorrow morning."

"We? As in you and me?" Her skin crawled. She had no wish to spend more time with him than absolutely necessary and she certainly didn't look forward to sitting several hours next to him on a train.

"Exactly. I want to make sure that you actually arrive at your destination this time."

Oh really? Wasn't it you who dragged me from the train? "How kind and thoughtful of you."

"Right?" He beamed with pride, oblivious to her sarcasm.

Zara didn't have the heart to disappoint him and nodded. In his warped mind he probably believed he was being a nice guy. Although she couldn't fathom why he wanted to be kind to her when his job description was to intimidate people.

"I'll leave you to wash up." He pointed to a hidden door beside the vanity and added, "There is a new dress for you too."

She looked down her body, taking in the disgusting blood-crusted rags that posed as a dress, and this time she was honestly grateful. "Thank you, that's really kind of you."

Sensing the change in her attitude he made a contented face and said, "If you need help washing up, I'll gladly do the honors."

Unsure whether he actually expected her to take him up on the offer, she quickly disappeared into the bathroom, relieved when she found that the door could be locked from the inside.

THE NEXT DAY he drove them to the station where they boarded a train to Fulda via Halle and Erfurt, since the direct route via Helmstedt/Marienborn was closed due to the Berlin blockade.

At first, she felt uncomfortable in his company. Despite his civilian clothes he looked the part of a Russian from a mile away. She threw hurried sideways glances at the other passengers, hoping none of them would consider them a couple, since the last thing she wanted was to be mistaken as a *Russenflittchen*, a girl who slept with the Russian oppressors.

But the longer the excruciatingly slow train travelled through the Soviet occupied zone, the more she got used to his presence and when the train was diverted to Leipzig where Soviet military police boarded and thoroughly searched all the passengers, she was actually grateful to have Captain Rublev by her side. It took him only a single barked sentence in Russian, waving his military badge, for them to leave the compartment without so much as glancing at her papers.

"That was quite impressive, Captain Rublev," she said in an attempt to break the uncomfortable silence between them. The journey would last the better part of the day and she might as well have someone to talk with.

"Comes with the job," he said. "I think we're way past formalities. I'm Vladimir." He stretched out his hand.

Zara hesitated a moment to take it. He was still a Russian. And she hated all Russians. But remembering her determination to stay on friendly terms, she shook his hand, saying. "Are we friends now, Vladimir Rublevitch?" He broke out into laughter, leaving her wondering what she had said that was so funny.

"I admit this is quite complicated for foreigners, but the correct way to address me would be Vladimir Alexandrovitch, since that is my father's name."

Zara nodded, not understanding anything. He picked up on her confusion and chuckled. "Just call me Vladi, will you?"

"Vladi it is then. I'm Zara by the way."

He laughed again and every time he did, he lost the intimidating aura about him. After a while he asked, "Why do you hate the Soviets so much?"

"Apart from the fact that they've been raping and torturing me, you mean?" She could see his ears burning bright and almost felt sorry for him. Almost, because he was a Russian and they didn't deserve her sympathy.

"I'm sorry for that. I certainly don't condone that kind of behavior. But just because we have a few bad apples doesn't mean our entire system is bad."

"Oh, if you're talking about Communism, I think it's just as bad as the Nazis were."

Vladi looked around, worry in his eyes, before resting his gaze on her again. "You shouldn't say those things out loud."

"See what I mean? You're not even allowed to speak your mind. Nobody is allowed to criticize Stalin or Communism. What does this have to do with the lie of democracy and freedom that your superiors want to sell us on?"

"We do have the liberty to speak our mind."

Zara couldn't fathom how this seemingly intelligent guy could rehash such garbage. "Tell that to the press and their lack of freedom."

He cast her an indulgent gaze. "It is a generally accepted, but wrong notion that the Soviet Union should not be a democracy because it lacks freedom of press. The opposite is true."

Then he launched into an explanation that sounded to Zara like a well-rehearsed speech, comparable to the role an actor played in the theatre. "Imperialist newspapers often claim that the Soviet press is controlled by the government, which obviously is completely wrong. See, there doesn't exist such a thing as an uncontrolled press, the sheer idea of its existence is absolutely ridiculous. It might have existed in previous centuries, when some small newspaper would write their own articles and distribute them on their own account. But these times are long over. In our modern world all media is controlled by someone."

That much Zara could agree with, but she was wary of giving him a sign of her agreement.

His voice became louder, more dogmatic as he continued to lecture her on the principles of free press. "Nowadays each and every major newspaper is owned by a company. In the capitalist world this company is owned by a capitalist businessman and the goal of the entire operation is to bring in profit."

"What's so bad about profit?" Zara asked. She had expected him to get riled up at her irreverent remark, but instead he grinned in that pretentious way of his and stood up to continue his lecture.

"That is a topic for its own discussion. For the moment suffice to say that in capitalist countries the profit controls what the press writes. In reality, the Western press is the enemy of the people, whereas in the Soviet Union it isn't. The newspapers are owned by the people and nobody else. Therefore, the press can never be in the situation of acting against the best interests of the people, who effectively own and control it."

"That's bullshit," Zara interrupted him, but he had talked himself into such a fervor he didn't notice her objection.

"The people of the Soviet Union own all the printing plants, the paper producing factories, the distributors, and even the shops that sell the newspapers. All the employees are part of the people. Therefore, whatever they write, they do it for their own interests and hence the written words always match exactly the interests of the people. Do you see?"

Zara did not. His arguments were the usual warped communist arguments that might make sense at the first glance but as soon as one stopped a moment to actually think, they fell apart like a house of cards.

She looked at him, wondering how he'd become so brainwashed to believe all this shit, then she had an idea. "Are you saying the employees of a Western newspaper don't belong to the people?"

He looked at her like she was some kind of extraterrestrial and sighed. "You really don't understand, do you? They may be part of the people, but they are controlled by capitalist owners, so they have to write for profit and not in the interest of the people."

Zara had to bite back a giggle. Vladi was delusional. "I think I get it now. But who is this mean-intentioned profit forcing the poor reporters to write against their own best interest?"

He cast her a doubting glance, apparently unsure whether she was serious or not. But before he engaged in another lengthy monologue about the benefits of freedom and democracy in the Soviet Union she stopped him with a wave of her hand. "It's such a lovely day, we shouldn't ruin it by talking about politics. Don't you think so?"

An exasperated sigh filled the air, but he sat down again and kept silent until Zara started asking him about the weather and climate in Moscow.

12

GLENN

G lenn got up from his bunk, tiredly rubbing his eyes. Once again, he'd barely slept all night, because flight crews had been coming and going constantly throughout the night. Most of the men tried to be quiet, but a dozen men walking into the barracks with their heavy boots, getting ready to sleep, was about as quiet as a herd of cows storming the place.

He envied those fresh and young men who could sleep through anything, since he'd lost this talent many years ago, during the war. As much as he loved the cowboy operation the airlift was, where he never knew what he'd be doing the next day, nor what schedule he'd be working on, or which aircraft he would be flying, he hated the fact that after a hard day's work, he didn't even know where to sleep.

Brigadier General John Smith, responsible for the airlift operations, was overwhelmed with men and machines coming in faster than he could organize food, accommodation or mechanics for them. But what had been a jolly game for the first days had soon transformed into a trudge, because Glenn wished nothing more than to return to base, fall on his bunk and get eight hours of shuteye before tackling another twelve hours of back-to-back flights. Instead, he had to hunt for a meal and an empty bunk to fall down on, and then was woken at least six times per night when other crews came in and did the same.

He was ready for some military discipline.

"Captain Davidson?" a young soldier asked him.

"Yes. Who wants me?"

"General LeMay wants to see you."

Glenn racked his brain wondering what the commander of the US Air Forces in Europe could want from him. He'd done nothing wrong, at least nothing that would warrant being cited to the highest command. A chill trickled down his spine as he remembered the night spent in the bed of a German Fräulein and returning to the garrison in the wee hours of the morning. But surely, this wasn't something LeMay would deal with personally?

"What's he want?" Glenn asked.

"Dunno. But he said it's urgent."

Glenn straightened the wrinkles in his uniform with his hands and took off to the administration building where the general's office was. The door stood wide open and LeMay waved him inside as soon as he saw him coming up. "Come in, I have been waiting for you."

"Yes, sir."

"General Harris called." LeMay didn't look too happy, and Glenn still couldn't figure out what all of this had to do with him. He stood at attention and waited, while looking around the general's office. The quarters of the occupation forces were the exact opposite of the temporary offices for the airlift operations. Everything in here reeked of an orderly, even lazy life, working several hours in the morning and spending the afternoons with representative tasks, also known as luncheons, shopping and get-togethers. A stark contrast to the hectic, chaotic and sometimes utterly enervating conditions for the airlift crews.

The general got up from behind his huge wooden desk and beckoned Glenn to follow him to the window of the corner office. Looking out, Glenn had a clear view to the tower and the landing strip. He could see the string of planes coming in from Berlin and those lined up on the ground waiting to take off.

But he also saw the many men milling about like ants. The entire airbase swarmed with activity, fuel trucks rushing back and forth, carts crisscrossing the airfield for loading the aircraft.

General LeMay took a deep breath and said, "General Harris has asked me to fly coal to Berlin."

"Sir? Did you say coal, sir?" Glenn suppressed the reflex to tear his eyes wide open. The general must know that this was impossible. Transporting coal by air was an outrageous undertaking that had never been tried before. And for good reasons.

"Yes. I told him if he can provide it, the Air Force can fly it."

Glenn's jaw dropped to the floor. Air saturated with coal dust was highly explosive. This was a common problem in the coal mines, where spontaneous combustion happened frequently.

Having coal on an airplane was a sure invitation for a nice explosion mid-air, and Glenn for one had no intention of being splattered into a million pieces.

"You came highly recommended by Harris, so I want you to do a test run." Glenn felt the blood draining from his face. He hadn't minded going up against a dozen German Messerschmitts during the war, but against the invisible enemy of dust saturating the air in his bird and possibly blowing the entire crew into obliteration? That was a completely different beast.

LeMay continued, while looking out at the airfield beneath them. "In order to minimize the risk and simplify unloading, one of the logistics men suggested dropping the coal from the bomb bays."

"Sir, with all due respect, do you want me to drop a load of coal onto the city of Berlin?"

"No, the test will be done at Rhein-Main Airport. A B-29 is waiting for you with loaded bomb bays. And since General Harris insisted you're the best pilot far and wide, you'll get to do the honors of the first test flight."

"Yes, sir." Glenn wasn't sure whether he should be proud to be called best pilot on the base or start cussing. He'd always wondered how the Japanese kamikaze pilots must have felt before leaving on a mission. Now he knew, and he didn't like it one bit. He might be crazy, but he loved to be alive. But refusing a direct order by General LeMay was out of the question.

With sagging shoulders, he found the B-29, and climbed into the cockpit to embark on the ten-minute flight to the neighboring airport. Since it might be his last one, he decided to enjoy the beautiful sunshine gleaming into the cockpit, painting brilliant glitter across the old and worn-out instruments.

That bird, like virtually all taking part in Operation Vittles, had definitely seen better times and was way past its natural life. Due to the rushed operation, aircraft had been called in from all four corners of Europe, some of them hastily patched up for their last flying adventure.

A smile crossed his face as he remembered the British saying *Mend and make do.* Yep, they were mending old veteran aircraft to tickle a few thousand more miles out of the spent machines. But his smile faltered the moment he approached an unused field behind the Rhein-Main airbase and he straightened his spine, giving one hundred percent attention to the task before him.

He took the B-29 lower and lower, beneath the treetops standing like wagging fingers in the distance. Once he distinguished the individual grass stalks, he engaged the bomb bay, while simultaneous pushing the speed to maximum and willing his bird to fly up and away like an agile fighter plane and not the slow Superfortress it was.

He heard the catastrophic explosion before he saw it. Beneath him the coal exploded and sent a darting flame into the air. Glenn believed he felt the heat engulfing his bird and pushed the engines to the limit, before he flew a curve and returned to look down at the drop site from a safe height. Way below him, fire workers rushed to the site, putting out the fires quickly eating away at the lush green grass.

After three more attempts with the same results, he returned to Wiesbaden to report on his mission. The general commented wryly, "I guess this type of bombing isn't as successful as our raids on Japanese cities were."

A wave of relief shot through Glenn's body at the abandonment of this undertaking, but LeMay quickly disappointed him, saying, "We'll have to find another way to transport the coal."

"Why do they need the coal so urgently, when it's summer and no need for heating?" Glenn later asked one of the logistics people.

The man rolled his eyes and explained that coal was needed mostly to generate power, to keep everything from light bulbs in apartments to the subway to industries going. Although he admitted that in winter there'd be a much higher need for coal, because it was used for heating, too. But by then, the airlift would long be history.

13

VLADI

When the train passed the inner German border Vladi switched his Red Army papers for those of a German businessman travelling to Frankfurt, since he didn't want to explain to the American military police what a captain of the Red Army was doing in their zone amidst their folly of an airlift to circumvent a siege that didn't exist.

He could only shake his head at the vile propaganda the Western newspapers spewed about the Soviets. They simply didn't want to understand that Berlin by right and heritage belonged to the Soviet Union and not to the lazy American, British and French Allies, who'd done next to nothing fighting Hitler, while the brave Soviet people and their great Red Army had borne the brunt of the fighting.

When the train finally arrived in Wiesbaden, he carried Zara's suitcase and jumped onto the platform, before helping her down.

"Will you find your way around?" he asked her. For some reason, he wanted to make sure she was safe here, but unlike in the Soviet zone, he didn't have the means to protect her against those thuggish Americans.

"I'm sure I'll be perfectly fine with the uncultivated Americans who kidnap women from the train to torture them," she said, a sardonic smile spreading across her lips.

She had the uncanny ability to make his blood boil with her smug reproaches of his people. Getting rid of her was for the best of everyone, and he actually looked forward to the havoc she'd wreak on the Americans should they interrogate her about her father's whereabouts.

"Call me when your father shows up," he said and handed her a piece of paper with a phone number in his department that was attended to day and night.

She stared at the white sheet, her cute face taking on an incredulous expression, before she stared at him with blank exasperation and said, "You don't actually expect me to call you, do you?"

He didn't answer. He was sure she'd come around and do what was best for her when her father showed up. Then he walked away.

Wiesbaden was very different from Berlin, which was still mostly in ruins. Here, it seemed, the ugly war had passed by without damage to the beautiful city. Everywhere he looked were beautiful villas with gardens around them, requisitioned by the occupying forces for their officers. He scoffed. How about democracy and freedom? Here in their zone the American capitalists showed their true colors, keeping the best housing for themselves, robbing the German civilians of what actually belonged to them, while accusing the Soviets of every crime under the sun, when all the Soviet Union wanted for Germany was reconciliation, and a peaceful life as a brother country in the vast communist empire.

He took out his map and searched the route to his next destination. Since he was already here, he wanted to make the best use of his time and visit Werner Böhm, the former chairman of the SED education and propaganda committee.

Böhm was a traitor to the Soviet Union, who'd defected about a year ago, and his escape from Berlin had caused quite the ripples among the communist apparatchik. His sheer existence was a smudge on the image of Communism and Stalin himself.

The NKVD, of course, was surveilling Böhm, but since he was under the protection of the Americans, who had welcomed the traitorous man with open arms, all their attempts to sequester him had been unsuccessful.

Vladi didn't delude himself into thinking he could single-handedly kidnap Böhm, but it wouldn't hurt to remind the man that his life was always in danger and he'd never be able to live in peace for as long as he defied the Soviet Union.

With a cigarette in the corner of his mouth, Vladi bided his time in front of the radio station where Böhm worked. He recognized the tall and slender man with the ash blond hair immediately and approached him.

"Comrade Böhm, may I have a word, please?" Vladi said in Russian.

Böhm looked over his shoulder, as if to make sure there weren't men in dark suits waiting for him, before he answered, "What do you want?"

"Just a little talking."

"Then you're not here to kidnap me?"

Vladi appreciated the up-front honesty and bit back a laugh. "Not today. But I want to make you an offer."

"An offer I can't refuse?" Böhm smirked.

Vladi showed his empty hands, pretending to be unarmed, despite the revolver in his shoulder holster and the knife pinned to his calf. In fact, he didn't even have an offer, but it was worth a try. If he could bluff Böhm into coming back to the Soviet zone with him, that would make the news and nobody would ever ask about Zara Ulbert again.

He still hadn't quite figured out how to explain that he'd let her go, but if he delivered Böhm to the high brass, that wouldn't be needed.

"Not this kind of offer. Can we go someplace?"

Böhm's face closed with suspicion and he glanced around.

"I am alone."

"Let's go to the café then," Böhm said and led the way to a small place with the very ingenious name *Der Backladen* — the baker's shop. It was nothing more than a bakery, one of the most ubiquitous shops in Germany, since the Germans lived and breathed for everything bread. Dark bread, white bread, rye bread, sweet bread, bread-like sweets, and more.

Vladi had never in his life imagined there could be hundreds of different types of bread and, naturally, every single bakery had a specialty with a secret recipe handed down for generations.

There were two small tables with chairs inside and five more on the outside. Böhm pointed to one of the tables on the outside, before asking, "Are you still with *them*?"

Vladi nodded, grateful that Böhm didn't mention his employer. Even though they were speaking Russian, someone might have understood them and he wasn't keen on anyone knowing his true identity.

"The order is on me. What do you want?"

Vladi looked at the display, his mouth watering at the sight of all those sweet delights. There was so much more choice than even the best-stocked occupation-forces-only shops in Berlin had to offer, let alone the shops anywhere in the Soviet Union. It occurred to him that maybe the American way of life wasn't all bad, and Böhm's decision to defect had actually served him well, but he pushed the thought aside. Things might look beautiful from the outside, but capitalism was ugly to those who had to live with it. Everyone knew that.

"Was möchten Sie?" The baker's wife interrupted his musings with her question about what he wanted. He chose a yummy-

looking *Rosinenbrötchen*, a sweet yeast bun with raisins, and coffee — real coffee. Then he waited for Böhm to pay, before they walked outside and settled at one of the small tables. Moments later, the baker's wife delivered their order to the table.

"So, what's your reason for being here, Captain Rublev?" Böhm asked.

The fact that he hadn't called him comrade instantly raised a red flag, meaning the other man had truly and finally broken with the communist ways. Out of malice, Vladi answered, "You are the reason, Comrade Böhm."

"I'm not your comrade anymore. If you want something from me, you'd better get this straight."

"Of course, Werner Paulevich." Vladi purposefully used a mocking tone as he twisted Böhm's name and used it in the traditional Russian manner.

Böhm scowled at him, but didn't object this time. Vladi observed the features of the other man for any hints, and then had a sudden inspiration. "Have you heard about SS-Obersturmführer Karl Ulbert?"

"The former Kommandant of Mauthausen? Who hasn't?" Böhm's face was a blank façade not giving away his real thoughts, a skill he'd developed going for years through the same grueling political training Vladi himself had endured. Böhm had been a master at wielding the word, which was why it had been an especially great disappointment when he defected and turned against the Soviet Union.

Vladi remembered how General Sokolov had been livid for weeks, hurling insults at anyone who had the misfortune to come near him following Böhm's clandestine escape from Berlin and his subsequent public condemnation of the Soviets and their way of Communism on the American radio.

He bit into his *Rosinenbrötchen,* which gave him valuable time to think about his next move. Heavenly sugary flavor exploded on his tongue. Taking his time, he carefully searched for words and then said, "There are rumors that he has surfaced and we are very much interested in finding him first."

"What does this have to do with me?"

"You must be aware that you're still on the most-wanted list and the NKVD is surveilling you, just waiting for an opportunity to sequester you away behind the Iron Curtain, Werner Paulevich."

Böhm looked as if he'd bitten into a lemon instead of an utterly delicious sweet pie, and Vladi noticed a slight tremble in the German's hand as he picked up his cup of coffee. An excited rush coursed through his veins and turned into a deep satisfaction, as he realized that Böhm definitely was aware of his precarious situation and would most likely be willing to consider Vladi's offer.

"I can help you," Vladi said, meeting Böhm's suspicious gaze as honestly as he could. "If you happen to hear about his whereabouts and let me know..." he pushed a card with the name and phone number of an agent in Wiesbaden across the table, "...your name will disappear from the most wanted list."

"Will it?"

"Yes, it will."

Böhm slowly shook his head. "I don't know anything."

"If you hear something, you know how to find me. The central committee is generous to those who support it." Vladi emptied his cup of coffee and stood up. "Thanks for the coffee."

14

ZARA

Zara stared at the paper Vladi had given her and crumpled it in her hand, intending to never look at it again. His arrogance was mind-boggling. After everything she'd endured at the hands of the Soviets, albeit not his, he actually believed she'd deliver them her father.

It wasn't that she was particularly fond of her father, since he'd left her to her own devices three years ago, but he was still family. Anyway, it was highly unlikely that he'd suddenly contact her after such a long time.

She took a deep breath, looking at the relatively undamaged city of Wiesbaden, which presented such a stark contrast to Berlin. Where the capital was destroyed, sad and gray, this town was intact, lovely and full of colors. Although now wasn't the time to reminisce. She squared her shoulders and took the handwritten directions from her purse, dropping the crumpled paper inside.

The drawn map in her hand, she left the *Bahnhofsplatz*, the square in front of the train station, and set out to find the house where she would be working for her new employers, the Gardners. But with each step her trepidation grew. What had seemed a perfect way to leave Berlin and start a new life in the American zone suddenly loomed like a monster in the distance.

Like a good German girl, she'd never had a professional education, and her only skills – child caring, sewing, stitching and cooking – didn't leave her with many choices. Disdain for her father and his Nazi ideology overcame her and she balled her hands into fists. Both her friends Marlene and Bruni had real jobs and real skills. Only she hadn't learned a single useful thing in the school for higher German girls and now had to work as housemaid.

Her parents had employed all kinds of domestic servants, maids, a cook, a gardener, a driver – she'd never once believed she would have to become one herself. So many things had changed since she was a sheltered society girl. She gritted her teeth, determined to decide upon her own fate from now on. She was forever done with being the good girl who catered to the wishes of everyone else.

Despite her pep talk, her courage sank with every step she was taking toward her destination. Mrs. Gardner didn't know she was coming. With Vladi's sudden decision to release her, she'd been too anxious to even consider calling ahead.

A frightening thought entered her mind. What if Mrs. Gardner already had found a new person to take care of the household and sent her away? Where would Zara stay? She didn't know anyone in Wiesbaden. The closest relative she had was in Saarbrücken, a town about one hundred miles south-west —in the French zone, for which she had no valid travel papers.

After a fifteen-minute walk she arrived in front of a strikingly beautiful house that reminded her of the villa her family had lived in during their time in Linz. Memories stormed her mind and made her feel so dizzy she had to lean against the white picket fence to steady herself.

Inside the garden with beautiful herbaceous borders in full bloom she saw a sandbox and a swing. All determination left her and she wanted nothing more than to run away. A broken person like her had no business staying in such an idyllic world. But just as she turned on her heel, a blond boy came storming toward her, yelling, "Hey, are you coming to visit my mom?"

His bright smile and the mischief written all over his face immediately eased her anxiety and she answered in her slightly rusty English, "Actually, I am. My name is Zara Ulbert, and I was supposed to come here a while ago."

His eyes opened wide. "You're our maid?" Without waiting for her answer, he rushed off, shouting at the top of his lungs, "Mommy, Mommy, the maid is here!"

Zara felt herself blushing, because at the volume of his shouts half the town must have heard his announcement, and she hated to be the center of attention. Her eyes darted around, looking for a place to hide from the invisible stares scrutinizing and judging her.

Moments later a petite brunette appeared, wearing a fashionable dark blue dress with short sleeves, padded shoulders and a belt around the waist. Her feet were stuck into red peep toe sandals with platform soles. Judging by the incredulous expression on her face this must be the mother of the boy, and Zara's employer.

"Mrs. Gardner? I am Zara Ulbert."

"We expected you weeks ago." Mrs. Gardner's voice was cold as ice, causing chills to rush through Zara's veins. This would never work out.

"I'm sorry, it's a long story. If you would let me explain, and maybe give me another chance?" At the scowl in Mrs. Gardner's face, Zara added, "That is, if you haven't employed someone else."

"No, we haven't. It's not so easy to find someone I can trust with my children."

Since the other woman didn't invite her in, Zara said, "I'm truly sorry. I appreciate the opportunity to work for you and was already on my way to Wiesbaden when Soviet military picked me off the train."

"We'd better go inside then."

Zara followed her to the beautifully furnished sitting room, and again she had the eerie feeling of being back in the family house in Linz. She had been very naïve back then, deliberately blanking out anything that didn't fit into her view of the world and believing if she didn't notice, it couldn't be there.

For years now, she had struggled with the guilt and shame of being complicit with the Nazis' crimes, and her father's in particular, because she had not actively resisted. She had taken her easy life for granted and had lived in that lovely house, so similar to this one, shielded from the truth of what was going on outside.

She shrugged off the guilt, pressing her lips into a truculent line. It wasn't as if she hadn't paid her dues – more than once. Now, she wanted to forget about the past and start a new life.

Inside, Mrs. Gardner offered her iced tea and asked her to sit down at the mahogany dining table. Zara took a sip and told her hopefully future employer about the Soviets and their interrogation, leaving out the gory details.

"But why would they do this? What have you done?" Mrs. Gardner asked suspiciously.

"It was about my father."

"Your father?"

Zara was surprised that Mrs. Gardner didn't know, since she had expected the Americans to run a background check on her. Apparently, they had been content with her denazification certificate. As much as she wished to keep this dark part of her family story a secret, she decided to come clean about her father's identity. How else could she explain the Soviets' interest in her?

"He was the Kommandant of the Mauthausen concentration camp and fled the country toward the end of the war. The Soviets believe he has resurfaced and were sure I knew his whereabouts. But I don't know anything. He hasn't contacted me. Even if he had, I would have sent him to hell. I don't want anything to do with him. He's a beast." She took a deep breath. "Please, you have to believe me. Since the day I was expelled from Austria and returned to Berlin, I have lived in fear of the Russians, and that's the reason why I left my hometown and came to the American zone. To feel safe again."

Mrs. Gardner nodded several times with a serious face, but never interrupted her. When Zara ended her story, she said, "I will have to talk with my husband about this. He'll be home in the evening." She gave Zara a scrutinizing look and then asked, "Do you have a place to stay?"

Zara hesitated a moment too long, and Mrs. Gardner said, "I see you don't. You can stay here until my husband has made his decision."

"Thank you so much, this is so very kind of you. Can I make myself useful meanwhile?"

"No need. Please come with me, I'll show you the guestroom where you can refresh meanwhile."

Zara must have been more tired than she admitted to herself, because she immediately fell asleep on the bed and woke up to a heated argument from the neighboring room. When she heard her name, she tiptoed to the wall and pressed her ear against it.

"Alright, she can stay. As long as she works hard and doesn't get into trouble."

"I'll see to that," Mrs. Gardner answered and then erupted into a soft giggle, "Not here. The children..."

Zara almost screamed with relief. She tiptoed back to the bed and then made a show of noisily getting up and walking with heavy steps to the door, making sure she was loud enough for the couple to hear her.

15

GLENN

Glenn eyed a battered aircraft that still showed the black and white marks identifying it as a veteran of the invasion in Normandy. That Gooney Bird had definitely seen better times, but beggars couldn't be choosers and with the raging scarcity of aircraft in airworthy condition, he would take anything with wings.

Just a few days ago, the required twenty-five-minute break between blocks had been slashed down to three minutes, against the objections of ground control. This had increased the number of planes in the air at any given time, but also stretched the capacity of the maintenance teams to extreme limits, turning finding a properly maintained aircraft into a veritable nightmare.

"Mind if I take that bird?" Glenn asked one of the mechanics on the airfield.

"If you have a rubber john," the mechanic answered.

"What?" Glenn looked incredulously at the man, who didn't give away any signs that he'd made a joke.

"We're short on rubber seals for the windscreen wiper

hydraulics, so we use a condom, but I'm out of them." He showed his empty hands.

Wordlessly Glenn reached into his breast pocket and fished out a package, dangling it in front of the mechanic. "But the bird is mine?"

"Sure is. Takes me two minutes to fix it and off you go." The mechanic tore the package open, cut off the condom's tip, rolled it onto the rubber ring for the hydraulics and said, "Seal's done. Won't last longer than two days, but better than nothing."

Glenn happily rushed toward the plane in an attempt to claim it before anyone else.

"But I have to warn you, this one's been overdue for both the twenty-five and two-hundred-mile checks," the mechanic shouted after him.

While the regular maintenance after every flight was more or less taken care of, most aircrafts hadn't been through their periodic inspections. As long as the thing flew, it was needed up in the air and not on the ground for a lengthy overhaul.

Glenn had always thought the maintenance people were making too much of a fuss about the periodic inspections, and the current situation showed that he was right. Aircraft were flying just fine, and it was more than enough to fix broken things instead of checking anything and everything just because the craft had been such-and-such number of hours in the air.

"What's that stuff?" Glenn asked one of the Germans loading the plane and pointed at the olive Army duffel bags, the exact same type that he lugged around containing his belongings.

"*Kohle.*"

"Coal? Which crazy nutjob has ordered us to transport coal in the cargo department of this craft?"

"I did." Glenn jerked around and stared directly into the face of a general.

"I'm sorry, sir."

Glenn felt his earlobes burning hot, but the general graciously ignored Glenn's disrespectful remark and added, "After the failed dropping experiments our logistics guys experimented with several forms of packaging. Turns out these duffel bags don't get as dirty as bags made of more porous material and there's significantly less coal dust in the air – definitely not enough to cause an explosion."

"Good to know, sir," Glenn said, but he still sensed an uncomfortable tickle in the back of his head at the thought of having to fly coal to Berlin.

Twenty minutes later, Glenn took off, his trusted copilot Teddy and a flight engineer called Gus with him. The weather was good, the visibility fantastic and Glenn thoroughly enjoyed the journey until they reached the air corridor through Soviet territory.

Flying through the twenty-mile wide corridor, while not exactly challenging, was always nerve-racking, since the underlying threat of some kind of stupid Soviet action was constantly there. The entire flight took only one and a half hours and they were quickly approaching Tempelhof Airport, when Glenn suddenly heard a strange rattle.

He took off his headset and said, "Shush. Do you hear that?"

All three men listened intently, and then Teddy said, "What the hell is it?"

"Not sure. Something loose." Gus crept into the cargo department to check for anything loose, but returned empty-handed. Meanwhile they arrived over Berlin and Glenn told Teddy to lower the landing gear, but the green light, indicating the gear was down and locked didn't light up.

"Shit, landing gear isn't locked," he said, well aware that a rough landing of an aircraft loaded to the brim with coal might well turn into a catastrophe.

"Probably a problem with the hydraulics." Gus had already got off his seat and reported back moments later, "I can fix it, but not in time for the landing."

Glenn radioed the tower about their problems and aborted the landing to go around and try again. After a while Gus said, "It should work now."

Dropping the gear again, Glenn noticed how the tension in his shoulders eased when the green light lit up fast and bright. He swiped his forehead and cursed beneath his breath. "Are they using condoms for the landing gear too?"

Both Gus and Teddy gave him uncomprehending stares.

"Forget about it..." On his way round, he saw the next aircraft in line being sent into a holding pattern until Glenn was down. Since landing was done in ninety-second intervals there wasn't much margin for error, so he swiftly proceeded with the landing procedures and this time he touched down like a feather.

After three round trips he was exhausted to the bone and all he wanted was a nice, hot shower and a long, uninterrupted sleep. But neither of those things happened. Another crewman told him he'd been to the shower rooms just to find out that all the hot water had been used up and it would take at least thirty minutes to heat again. Glenn had the choice between waiting or showering ice-cold, which would do nothing for his aching muscles and bring him wide awake. He opted to forego showering completely and instead get some decent sleep. But to add insult to injury, he found another man in his bunk and cursed a blue streak while searching for an empty bunk to drop down into.

16

ZARA

Zara came downstairs early to start her work, to find Mrs. Gardner already in the kitchen, preparing breakfast. "Please, let me help you, Mrs. Gardner."

"Call me Cath, everyone else does."

"Cath." Zara still had to get used to the informal attitude of the Americans. In a German household a servant would never, even after decades of service, call the lady of the house by her first name. "Thank you again for the opportunity, I will not disappoint you."

"I'll show you everything today and starting tomorrow you can work on your own."

After Mr. Gardner had left for work, Zara asked, "May I place a phone call to Berlin to let my friends know that I arrived safely at your house?"

"Off course. Please make it short." Cath showed her the black apparatus in the hallway and then left. Zara's best friend Marlene didn't have a phone at home, so she dialed Bruni's number, but it never connected. It didn't even ring. Next she tried Bruni's workplace, the Café de Paris. Even though it didn't open until afternoon, there were always staff cleaning and cooking. But it didn't ring either.

"Did you talk to your friend?" Cath asked when Zara returned to the kitchen.

"Unfortunately not. I tried at work and at home, but both lines are dead."

"That's strange. I'll ask Charles when he comes home. Maybe you could send her a letter instead," Cath suggested.

"I will. What do you want me to do right now?"

"Let me show you where we buy our groceries and everything else we need. After that we have to clean the house and attend to the garden. In the afternoon, I'll pick up John from school, and Lisa from kindergarten."

Zara nodded and put on her shoes. Cath had adopted the German habit of not entering the house with outside shoes, and kept slippers near the entrance, insisting nobody, not even guests, enter her house without putting the slippers on first.

Cath handed a basket to Zara and off they went to the grocery store. The area where the Gardners lived had stores for all essential goods nearby – most importantly a bakery, a grocery and a haberdashery. Zara found it easy enough to memorize the way.

"I like to buy here, because the produce is fresh and the locals give me a good price. But everything they don't have, I'll buy at the PX store."

Zara's head was whirling with the flood of new information. Grocery store, laundry, seamstress, and whatnot. It seemed Cath had a shop or a helper for everything. The grocer greeted them ebulliently and Cath introduced Zara, "Herr Schweigert, this is Fräulein Ulbert, our new housemaid. From now on she will be doing the shopping for me, so I hope you'll give her the same service as you've given me."

Herr Schweigert nodded with a serene expression. "Certainly, Mrs. Gardner. Your business is important to us."

As they exited the shop, Cath said, "I'm convinced he over-charges me, but at least he always keeps things hidden under the counter for me that he knows I want to buy."

Zara had already noticed that Herr Schweigert changed the prices according to the wealth of his customers, but she preferred not to say so.

Cath glanced at her watch and said, "We have about an hour before we have to fetch the children. How about I invite you for coffee and a pastry?"

"That would be nice, thank you very much." Zara couldn't quite believe her good luck. She'd not had a pastry in what seemed like years. The displays here in the small town of Wies-baden were so much more diverse than in Berlin, where you rarely saw anything other than bread, except if you were an Allied soldier and could pay with hard currency. For those customers the Berlin shopkeepers bent down deep below the counter and came up with the treasures hidden for the wealthy.

Zara had fully expected Cath to pay for the *good stuff* in US dollars, and was quite surprised that this wasn't the case. Every-where they went, the new Deutsche Mark was readily accepted. It fast became clear why the Soviets were so enraged about the currency reform, since their ruble had been a worthless piece of paper for a long time already, and now their hastily intro-duced East Mark would suffer the same fate.

Cath and Zara entered a small bakery called *Der Backladen* with several tables on the outside that seemed to cater exclu-sively to American military wives and their company. They settled at one of the tables, drinking their coffee and enjoying the warm sunshine, when Cath said, "I'll get another sweet pie for Charles, will you wait for me, please."

Zara jumped up. "I can get it for you."

"No worries, today is your first day. And besides, you don't know what he likes best."

While she was waiting for Cath, two American soldiers

strolled over and took the table next to hers. Predictably, both men sized her up and she inwardly shook her head at their cocky arrogance, believing every girl would fall over herself just to spend time with them. Not her. They might not be awful like the Soviets, but she had had enough of soldiers for the rest of her life.

She had to admit that the taller one of them with dark, short, yet tousled hair and a stubble forming on his jaw looked ruggedly handsome. He called out to her, "Why so alone, *schönes Fräulein?*"

Zara turned her head away, rolling her eyes at his antics, and was glad to see Cath exiting the bakery with a paper bag in her hand.

"Shall we leave?" Zara asked, eager to get away from the flirting soldiers. Handsome or not, she was not in the market to find a man, much less one of the occupying power.

But before Cath could answer, the handsome guy stood up and approached their table. "Cath! How are you?"

Zara bit down the groan erupting from her throat, while her employer warmly greeted the stranger, "Glenn. What are you doing here? Are you on leave again?"

"On the contrary, I'm finally getting some serious flying done with that Berlin thing. I should have called Charles, but you can't imagine how busy it is. Today is my first day off to explore the city." He glanced at Zara and his chocolate-brown eyes twinkled with mischief as he added, "And the beautiful sights it offers."

"That's lovely, Charles will be delighted. Why don't you come over on the weekend?"

"I'd love to. I'll check my schedule and let Charles know." He shook Cath's hand and then turned toward Zara to give her an absolutely devastating grin that made her skin tingle. "And who are you? A friend of Cath?"

"I am the housemaid," Zara said, putting as much ice into

her voice as she was capable of. Hopefully he'd have enough decency not to flirt with his friends' servant.

"Very pleased to meet you. What was your name again?"

Zara glared daggers at him, but couldn't well be rude to him in Cath's presence, so she answered. "Zara Ulbert."

"Zara, such a beautiful name."

The puppy look in his eyes softened Zara's resolve to dislike him and she said, "Thank you."

Then he turned around to walk away and Zara caught herself staring at his very muscular behind as he sauntered the few steps to his own table.

"We should go and fetch John from school." Cath got up, stowing the paper bag in the basket. They walked through streets with nicely tended gardens around the detached houses, which seemingly all belonged to the occupying forces.

Without warning, Cath remarked, "I really like him. He's one of Charles' best friends, but I must warn you he's both reckless and an incorrigible charmer."

It took Zara a few moments to grasp that Cath was talking about Glenn. A surge of warmth coursed through her veins at the well-meant advice, because it had been such a long time since someone other than Marlene and Bruni had actually cared about her.

Cath was being much too nice to her, kinder than Zara's own mother had ever been. Zara's eyes swam and she furtively blinked the forming tears away. After a stroll through the neighborhood they arrived at the garrison and Zara waited outside the compound for Cath to pick up her children.

She didn't mind sitting on a bench in the sun, but what she did mind was the myriad of American soldiers coming and going, because each and every one tried to hit on her. Even in Berlin the GIs, who were known for wanting to have a good time, had never been this annoying. But then there were plenty of women and comparatively few GIs in Berlin, as opposed to the ratio in this sleepy little town with its buzzing airbase.

"May I sit down?" She already had a scathing rebuke on the tip of her tongue, but since the voice sounded awfully familiar, she looked up and, of course, looked into Glenn's grinning face.

She bit her lips, torn between wanting to give him a piece of her mind and the need to be polite, because he was a friend of her employers.

He lowered his voice to a seductive whisper, "If I'm sitting here, nobody else will bother you. Your choice!"

She glowered at him, but nodded. "Be my guest."

He took a place beside her on the bench, carefully keeping an appropriate distance between the two of them and said, "Such a charming young lady. Would you do me the honor of going out with me?"

"No!" Zara wished she could show her sharp claws like a cat to let him know exactly what she thought about his advances.

"I thought so."

She looked at him, dumbfounded. "Then why did you even ask?"

"Can't hold it against a guy for trying, now can you?"

She cocked her head to the side and despite her best intentions to be terse with him, she had to smile. "I guess not."

"You're from Berlin, right?" he leaned against the backrest, seemingly without a care in the world.

"Yes." Zara had no intention of talking about the city she'd come to hate so much.

"The Gardners were expecting you a month ago, what happened?"

"None of your business," she snapped. Rage, hurt and pain attacked her out of the blue and she suddenly was back in the U-Boot with her interrogator about to hit her. The air became suffocating and she couldn't breathe anymore. Gasping, she stared at Glenn, who swam before her eyes taking turns in looking like her father, Captain Grusow, the other brutes who'd tortured her, and Vladi.

"Are you okay?" he sprang up, the concern in his voice making him look like himself again.

"I...I...can't breathe." Her vision clouded and suddenly everything was black. When she came to, she lay flat on her back, her legs propped up, Glenn bent over her. She almost fainted again at the thought that while putting her into this position, he must have gotten a good look at her knickers.

His face was so close to hers, she sensed his warm breath caressing her cheek. The intimacy of the situation scared her, but before she could say a word, he retreated and explained, "You fainted. I had to catch you or you would have dropped to the ground."

"Thank you." Her head was dizzy, but life was slowly returning to her bones. "I'd better..."

His hands softly pushed against her shoulders to make her lie still. "You should lie down a few more minutes. Shall I get you a doctor? I can rush into the garrison..."

"No, no need. I just fainted, it's not like something terrible happened." She wrapped her fingers around his wrists still resting on her shoulders and pushed him away before she sat up. "Thank you, I am fine."

He didn't answer, but his eyes filled with blank horror and she followed the direction of his stare to see her exposed thigh, which was covered with black, blue and green bruises. "Who did this to you?"

Shame burned through her veins, because he was the last person she wanted to know the truth. It was a topic she had no intention of ever talking about again.

"I fell down the stairs," she lied. "Really, it's nothing." She quickly smoothed down her skirt to cover the bruises.

His expression clearly indicated he didn't believe her, but nonetheless, he agreed, "As you say." Then he produced a chocolate bar from his pocket and offered it to her. "To get your strength back."

In a world deprived of precious sweets, the last thing she would do was to reject chocolate, so she gracefully took it. "Thank you very much." She took a hearty bite and soft sweetness with a hint of bitter exploded on her tongue. The chocolate melted against her gums and she couldn't help but close her eyes with delight. A soft chuckle made her open them in shock.

"Looks like you enjoy your chocolate. If you agree to go out with me, I can certainly get you more of it."

All the goodwill he had accumulated by helping her vanished within the blink of an eye. "I'm not for sale. Ever." She jumped up, ready to stomp off, when she remembered she had to stay and wait for Cath. "Dammit," she cursed beneath her breath.

Thankfully Cath returned at that moment with her children. Grateful for the opportunity to get away from Glenn, Zara rushed toward them.

"I'm sorry it took so long, but the teacher wanted to talk to me." Cath sighed. Judging by John's defiant face it was obvious he'd been the reason for this talk.

Zara, though, couldn't care less and spent the rest of the afternoon with the children in the garden on the swing and tossing a ball, deliberately shutting Glenn out of her thoughts.

17

GLENN

Rumors abounded that a new commander for Operation Vittles would arrive soon. After weeks of great fun and greater chaos, Glenn was ready for structure and hoped it would be someone experienced in the logistics of air operations.

But he didn't pay much attention to this issue, because he had a more personal problem, one he'd never experienced before and that irked him no end. He'd set his eyes on the beautiful Zara, but despite sending signals that she found him attractive, she showed him the cold shoulder.

Normally, the chase after a hard-to-get woman gave him pleasure, but with her it was outright frustrating. He'd pulled every trick in his playbook to get her to agree to a date with him, had even resorted to coaxing and bribery, but nothing had worked.

Pursuing Zara was already hurting his reputation as an irresistible womanizer. His pals had caught on and their teasing was relentless. But he was too stubborn to move on to greener pastures. He'd show the world that no woman could resist him. Not even Zara. His visits with Charles had become a frequent, barely veiled excuse to see her and the glances full of desire she threw at him, whenever she felt unobserved, spurred him on in his mission to conquer that woman.

He was standing in front of the mirror, shaving extra carefully, when several of his fellow airmen stepped inside the shower room.

"Never seen you shave in the afternoon. Still after that elusive Fräulein?" Teddy teased him.

"Shut up," Glenn snapped.

"Oh-oh. Someone needs to score urgently."

"Shut up," he growled and jerked his head around, cutting himself in the process. "Dammit! Look what you've done!"

Teddy laughed. "You've done that to yourself, you lovesick puppy."

If the insult hadn't come from his good friend he'd have grabbed the man by the throat. Now, he merely uttered a string of swear words.

SEVERAL DAYS LATER, with Zara foremost on his mind, Glenn was walking across the airfield, when he saw a brand-new Skymaster land. It was such a majestic bird, he had to stop and watch it roll across the landing strip. Deep in his heart, he was still a fighter pilot, but he'd dump the old Gooney Bird any day for one of these beauties.

He lingered to see it come to a standstill and almost toppled over when the door opened and a man in his forties, slim and wiry, with brooding eyes, the combed-back dark hair showing a receding hairline, stepped out. The man was by no means handsome, but emanated an impressive presence. Glenn didn't need to have a look at the insignia to know who it was. General Tunner was a legend.

While he'd never served under him, he'd crossed paths

with Tunner several times throughout his career and admired him for the clockwork-like efficiency he'd imposed on *The Hump*, the most famous airlift in the history of mankind. For three years, the operation had successfully supplied Chiang Kai-shek and the US Air Force in China in their fight against the Japanese. If Tunner was here, that Berlin thing was going to become serious business.

The glorious cowboy days of Operation Vittles would soon be over, transformed into a well-oiled machine. It would mean regular rosters, days off, always a hot shower and a bed to sleep in. Yes, Glenn had definitely grown tired of the unpleasant side effects of this Berlin adventure.

Two weeks in, on Friday the thirteenth of August, a godawful day, it was pelting cats and dogs from the sky and Glenn was called into General Tunner's office.

"Captain Davidson?"

"Yes, sir."

"I want you to fly me to Berlin."

"Now?" Glenn couldn't help but ask. It was the worst possible weather, scudding black clouds hanging low in the sky and torrential rain pouring down on Wiesbaden.

"We will start in an hour."

"Yes, sir." Together they walked to the flight office, to get the latest weather information. It wasn't good. Visibility was low on the entire route, although by now Glenn knew the route like the back of his hand and flying by instruments was a no-brainer. The one thing that worried him, though, was the landing. Tempelhof lay smack dab in the center of the city and at least one pilot had scraped the five-story buildings next to the airfield with his wings during a failed landing approach.

The flight office door opened and Glenn recognized the man who entered as one of the airport engineers, Victor Richards, and wondered what he was doing in the flight office.

"Richards, this is Captain Davidson, he'll run us up to

Berlin," Tunner said.

Glenn seemed to notice a flicker of fear in Richards' eyes and sure enough, the other man asked, "Is it even possible to fly in this weather?"

Glenn broke out in a huge grin. "Sure is. We will be number twelve in the block. Better get going."

Outside a lake was forming where a runway should have been. Glenn didn't mind rain. He knew that as long as there wasn't heavy mud on the ground, the aircraft would muddle through. He was more worried about the low-hanging impenetrable gray clouds. Soup, to be more correct. Very thick soup.

Teams of drenched and miserable German workers were getting the aircraft, lined up like a string of beautiful white pearls, ready for take-off. Equally drenched airmen boarded their birds, waiting for the next scheduled block, when they'd all take off at ninety-second intervals.

Tunner nodded and turned to leave the flight office. Glenn hurried to fall in step with him, while Richards followed them, seemingly reluctant, at a slight distance.

"Flying in blocks really has made a difference to efficiency," Glenn said to Tunner.

"Yes, it has, along with stacking in five levels, which increased the capacity of the air corridors."

"It's a shame though that the faster planes have to fly at the same speed as the slower ones. We could shorten air time and have more craft flying throughout the day if everyone flew as fast as they can."

Tunner shook his head. "What we gain in speed, we lose in chaos. As soon as aircraft have to overtake each other there will be chaos and trouble. Believe me, it's not worth it. The entire operation has to go steadily and evenly, almost as if on a conveyor belt."

Glenn personally didn't agree, and flying at the limit was so much more fun, but he'd never dare to contradict the general.

They hopped into the waiting car, and Glenn felt the familiar giddiness coursing through his veins. It was a thrill like no other to enter the cockpit of an aircraft and take the yoke in his hands, but this day he was doubly excited, because it was the first time he'd fly this brand-new Skymaster.

He taxied the Skymaster to the inundated runway, taking his place in the line of birds waiting to take off, and issued a warning to his crew and Richards to buckle in, because it was going to be a rough ride. So far, the weather wasn't that bad, despite the heavy rain, but news had come in that the conditions had worsened over the Harz Mountains.

For a moment he thought it might be wiser to abort the flight, but a sideways glance at General Tunner told him that was not the plan. Moments later the tower announced they were doubling intervals between take-offs. Glenn muffled a curse. Waiting was one of his least enjoyable occupations.

Finally, the wait ended, and as soon as they were given the go, his co-pilot Teddy pushed the throttles forward and the powerful engines came alive. It was the most exhilarating feeling in the world, and Glenn savored the moment when the force of acceleration pressed him back into his seat.

The roaring noise of the engines deafened him and the big aircraft shuddered like a freezing child, but suddenly the shudder smoothed out and, almost imperceptibly, the Skymaster raised its nose and took off into the skies. A smell of raw fuel wafted through the cabin, filling it with a sense of freedom, as Glenn took the big bird above the clouds, looking down at the cotton balls beneath him.

A long string of C-54s were headed along the same route, exactly three minutes apart from each other, each proceeding at exactly one hundred eighty miles per hour. Like a conveyer belt, just as General Tunner had envisioned it. Operation Vittles had indeed become an efficient clockwork.

Every three minutes another craft announced its exact time

loud and clear as it passed the Fulda beacon and entered the air corridor. Everything was running like a charm, despite the gray soup surrounding them.

But the moment Glenn reached the Harz Mountains, everything turned to hell. He saw the areas of turbulence, even before they grabbed his Skymaster and violently tossed it around. Holding on for dear life, he clasped his hands around the yoke to hold the heavy bird on a steady course.

Moments later they reached Soviet territory and from then on it would be tortuous maneuvering, because in the corridor he had no chance to circumvent bad weather zones. Glenn personally didn't mind, but he felt the heavy responsibility for his passengers on his shoulders – foremost General Tunner, since he had no intention of going down in history as the pilot who killed the Airlift commander during a crash, but also for Victor Richards, who was white as a ghost and looked ready to puke at any moment.

Glenn motioned to his flight engineer to go and look after their airsick passenger, while the fully loaded Skymaster was rolling, bumping, tossing and bucking. His focus was to keep them inside the twenty-mile-wide corridor, since he didn't want to imagine what might happen should they be blown out.

The Soviets had been playing hardball for quite a while, harassing American planes with their fake training maneuvers on the ground, shooting flash grenades, or buzzing the slow cargo planes with fast and agile Yak fighters. Nobody knew if they would take the gloves off and actually shoot down an American aircraft.

Glenn would rather not find out. Being downed behind enemy lines was the worst nightmare of any aircrew and even though the Soviets officially continued to be their allies, being stranded in their zone was as good as going down in enemy land as far as Glenn was concerned.

Meanwhile, in Berlin the ceiling had fallen in and

Tempelhof was shrouded in thick clouds, so low they touched the high buildings surrounding the airfield.

Tunner announced, "Tell Tempelhof air control that I want to try out ground-controlled approach."

A perfect day for this, Glenn thought. Ground-controlled approach, or GCA, was still in the experimental stage and had not been fully developed. Like most of the pilots Glenn had a love-hate relationship with the guys from ground control. On the one hand he prided himself on being able to fly and land in any weather, but truth be told, in a foggy soup like today GCA was actually the only way to safely set down a bird – if it worked.

"Shit," muttered Glenn as Tempelhof informed all approaching aircraft that two planes departing from the British airport at Gatow had lost their way and drifted into the Southern corridor with the incoming planes. The routes to and from Berlin had been set up as one-way operation: the Northern corridor was reserved for planes coming from the British airbases in the northern part of Germany and the southern corridor for the Big Easy planes coming in from the bases in the American zone, while the central corridor was used for everyone's journey home.

Glenn peered through his rain-washed windshield, hoping this one had a proper rubber seal and wasn't functioning with a condom that might not endure the heavy duty. But there was nothing to be seen ahead. Just thick, gray soup.

"Zero visibility," he said into his headset and, after orders from the tower, took the aircraft higher, flying circles over Berlin. Several minutes later the all-clear came through the intercom as ground control announced they had successfully talked down the first three Big Easy craft.

The new technology seemed to be working wonders and Glenn felt a jolt of relief. He actively released the tension from his muscles, rolled his shoulders and turned his neck.

"Big Easy four missed his approach and has to go around. Every Big Easy continue to fly waiting circles in the holding pattern," came the order from ground control and the tension returned with a vengeance. The usually short journey had turned into a hellish nightmare.

It seemed even the GCA guys struggled with the deteriorating conditions and bad news after bad news reached the planes still in the air. One Skymaster overshot the runway and crashed into the ditch at the end, where it caught fire. Another one landed too far down and had to brake with brutal force to avoid crashing into the burning wreck, causing his tires to go up in blue flames, while a third aircraft mistook an unfinished auxiliary runway for the real one and ground-looped before it came to a standstill.

Glenn strained his eyes, because surely, the fire could be seen, but there was nothing. It was exasperating to rely solely on the GCA without even the faintest vision. In the Berlin airspace, a circle with a twenty-mile radius above the city, planes were stacked from three thousand to twelve thousand feet.

When he received the command to fly into a space at eight thousand feet, which was reserved for General Tunner, while everyone behind him had to climb to the top of the stack, he was actually grateful for the general's presence. The Skymaster bucked around in the gale-force winds and he had his hands full keeping it on position. The ether was filled with constant chatter from the circling pilots, desperately calling for guidance.

"If anyone veers out of the holding pattern, we'll soon have a crash," he said to General Tunner, who looked sourer with every passing minute.

"The crew got out alive," ground control announced, and everyone in the cockpit, save for Glenn himself, who kept the yoke in a fierce grasp, broke out into cheers. But despite this good news, the situation was getting completely out of hand, since for the time being no more aircraft could land or take off, effectively clogging up airspace and ground space. Every minute they circled in this soup of fog filled with invisible, plane-shaped noodles in it increased the risk of a midair crash.

This was supposed to be a routine flight. Ninety minutes in. Touch down. Unload. Ninety minutes out. He checked the fuel. Going low. The next block coming in from Frankfurt was already passing the Fulda beacon and would soon be breathing down their necks, adding another twenty aircraft to the stack.

"This is a hell of a way to run a railroad," General Tunner suddenly snapped.

Glenn was wise enough not to respond, although he felt the general's despair deep in his own bones. Was this fateful Black Friday the day when the airlift ended for good? It had been a great effort while it lasted, but even before the feared winter approached, the Soviets seemed to flaunt the pact they'd made with the weather and were surely laughing their asses off while watching the helpless American aircraft struggling with squalls and clouds.

It was a cruel irony of fate, because as Glenn had discovered, General Tunner's main reason for visiting Berlin had been to attend a ceremony honoring the efficient and smooth-running Operation Vittles. During the ceremony he'd been supposed to award the pilot who had flown the most missions to Berlin, a Lieutenant Paul O. Lykins, with a valuable pocket watch, gifted by a grateful Berliner.

Now it looked disconcertingly as if General Tunner wouldn't be able to touch down and attend this celebration, where an estimated ten thousand people, Americans and German alike, were waiting for him. The infamy of being the pilot responsible for this propaganda disaster caused goosebumps to break out on Glenn's skin. He knew he'd be the target of mockery from his buddies for being a party-pooper.

"It's so damn embarrassing. The commander of the Berlin airlift can't even get himself into Berlin," General Tunner snarled and a hot twinge of guilt stabbed at Glenn, even though he knew, on a rational basis, that it wasn't his fault they were caught in this damn stack.

"Sir, we need to get them all down now or..." Glenn said after a while. Under normal circumstances, flying in stacks wasn't a problem, because there was enough space away from the airfield for any amount of aircraft to do their waiting circles, and even if this area overflowed, the tower could always allocate another one. But not here, since Berlin was an island in Soviet occupied territory and the only airspace available were the three corridors plus a twenty-mile circle over the city itself. All these aircraft circling in the foggy soup right now either had to land...or return to where they came from.

"Or what?" General Tunner responded.

"Or this will become a downright mess. The next block of thirty planes coming from Wiesbaden will be here in less than five minutes and then a mid-air collision is almost guaranteed."

Tunner didn't answer, but about ten seconds later he picked up the microphone and spoke with a calm but loud voice. "This is Big Easy twelve. General Tunner talking, and you listen. Send all Big Easy aircraft except for Big Easy twelve back to their base."

There was a long silence in the ether, before the tower responded, "Please repeat."

"I repeat. Send every single Big Easy over Berlin or in the corridor home. Then tell me when it's safe to land."

"Roger, sir," the man in the tower answered.

Glenn looked at the general in shock at this bold move. Ten minutes later ground control safely talked them down to the Tempelhof Airport, and Glenn had never been more relieved to step out of a cockpit.

18

VLADI

All day he'd spent outside in torrential rain and was drenched to his bones. His foul mood accurately matched the awful weather, as he kicked a few pebbles ahead of him. Snooping around the Wiesbaden airfield had been a complete loss of time.

He hadn't been able to smuggle himself inside the security area, and the only thing he saw was the runway slowly turning into a muddy lake. Not nearly enough intelligence to justify a day out in the rain. He decided to call it a day and return to his accommodations, where he'd phone in to his office and report the non-news.

But when he walked away, something unusual caught his attention. He couldn't quite put his finger on it, but it was odd. The hustle had decreased and the airfield seemed so...empty. Empty?

Looking up into the sky, he connected the dots. For a while, planes had been taking off like clockwork, but no landings had taken place, sweeping empty the murky waters posing as a landing strip.

The planes must be stuck in Berlin, probably due to bad

weather. Yep, the planes were stuck in Berlin and couldn't return for more cargo. He punched his fist into the air. *Serves them right, bloody imperialists.* Perhaps now they would accept the futility of their endeavor. If they couldn't even lick it during summer, they had no prayer to hope of continuing flying during the cold season.

He was basking in the glory of the great Soviet Union and how she would defeat her worst enemy, when he heard the droning of planes coming in from Berlin. One after another landed, and he didn't have to be an aviation expert to see they were heavy, loaded to the brim. He pressed his nose against the fence surrounding the airfield to get a better view. The scene unfolding in front of him confirmed his hunch: none of the planes taxied over to the cargo stations. The German workers stood motionless under the roof instead of rushing to the planes and loading them.

Since no more starts were carried out, the empty airfield kept filling with more and more aircraft, looking like a confused behemoth bereft of its only reason to exist. He cheered the bad weather, which had managed to delay the otherwise so efficiently working airlift.

Nobody in the Kremlin had expected those stubborn Americans to stick with this aimless endeavor for such a long time. It already approached the two-months mark and people in Moscow were beyond furious. They couldn't understand why the Americans wouldn't accept that it was better for everyone if the Soviets had sovereignty over all of Berlin, instead of clinging to their sorry boroughs like a cat about to fall out of a tree.

Stalin had been so confident after the war that the Americans would be in a hurry to send their boys home, leaving the European continent to the Soviet influence. He'd been wrong. A shiver ran down Vladi's spine the moment he realized what he had been thinking: Stalin was never wrong. If anyone ever found out Vladi's doubts, he'd disappear from the face of the earth faster than he could blink.

He gazed one last time at the grounded planes and then walked back to his shabby hotel on the outskirts of Wiesbaden. Since that damn currency reform, another evil feat of the horrible imperialists, the quickly introduced East Mark had plummeted in worth and the going exchange rate for the West Mark was around one to four – if anyone was even willing to exchange it.

The plentiful nice hotels in Wiesbaden were way above his budget and to add insult to injury, they flat-out refused to accept his emergency funds in rubles. The plump and drab receptionist had looked at him with a pitying glance, when she'd told him, "You'll soon find a job over here and lead a better life."

He'd wanted to slap her for her impertinence. In the Soviet zone he'd have her arrested for her crimes, but here he only felt humiliated, like a second-class citizen. Which was one more reason to hate the vicious capitalists. In the Soviet Union all people were equal, and nobody was judged by how much money they earned, while here, a man without money was worth less than a stray dog.

"Good evening, Herr Schmidt," the receptionist greeted him with another pitying glance as he entered the guesthouse looking like a drenched rat.

He wouldn't waste his charms on her, since he preferred his women lithe and energetic, with a streak of natural elegance. Out of spite he took off his hat in a swift movement, sending droplets all over the guest book on her counter. When she gave him an angry stare, he said, "I'm sorry, Fräulein. It's raining as if there was no tomorrow." Hopefully there wouldn't be a tomorrow for the ridiculous Operation Vittles.

With a smug smile he crossed the shabby entrance hall, relishing the knowledge that he was leaving a path of muddy shoeprints on the white linoleum and that witch behind the counter would have to mop the floor after he disappeared upstairs.

He unlocked the door and entered his room. It was small and worn-down, but clean and tidy. As much as he hated to admit it, even this shabby guesthouse offered more comfort than a normal hotel in the Soviet Union did. Flopping on the small bed, he propped up his shoes on the footrest and lit a cigarette. Smoking always helped him to think. He inhaled deeply, his eyes staring at the white ceiling, without seeing anything. General Sokolov had been so pleased with the results of the mini-airlift, the so-called milk run in April. Nobody in their wildest dreams had expected that the Americans would attempt to provide for an entire city by air.

When they did, it had been brushed off as a desperate gesture to buy goodwill with the German population and enough time to remove their troops without losing face. He took a furious drag on his cigarette and dipped the ashes into the ashtray on the nightstand. *To hell with these Americans!*

Nothing had worked according to plan. They were almost two months into the traffic controls and still no sign of them giving up. Two weeks prior, highly praised General Tunner had arrived and whipped Operation Vittles into unprecedented efficiency. Daily tonnages had crept up at a frightening rate since the very moment that vicious man had arrived in Wiesbaden.

Despite having spies counting the planes landing both at Tempelhof and Gatow airports, the Soviets had also positioned their people on the inside, working as cargo staff at the major airbases in both the American and British zones, where everyone could see the daily tonnage numbers written with chalk on oversized blackboards. Those workers confirmed what the numbers of the plane-counters hinted at, and it was nothing to be happy about.

He jumped up from his bed, stubbed out the cigarette and

put on his wet coat and hat before he rushed downstairs. Eyeing the pay telephone next to the reception, he walked out into the pelting rain once again. What he had to say should better not be overheard by anyone.

"Propov," answered his boss.

"Comrade Propov, this is Vladimir Rublev."

"Where the hell have you been?" Propov hollered.

Vladi raised a brow, Propov himself had sent him to go after Zara. "Following Zara Ulbert, as you ordered, Comrade."

"I wanted you to kidnap and interrogate her. How long can this take?"

"She didn't know where her father is, but..." Vladi desperately needed something to put his boss into a better mood. "... she agreed to cooperate and contact us if her father shows up, in exchange for our letting her go."

"You let her go? You're stupid, Rublev! Your weakness for beautiful women will one day be your downfall. I hope she was worth it."

Since Propov assumed he'd used Zara for pleasure, it was probably the best not to contradict him. Abusing a woman wasn't a crime he might be punished for; letting her go free, though, was. "I followed her to Wiesbaden and had a chat with Wolfgang Böhm."

"Böhm! That reprehensible man! Are you trying to make yourself dispensable?"

"On the contrary. He's in thick with the Americans and has an important position as advisor on Soviet relationships—"

"We know all this!" Propov hollered.

"He also sits on the editorial board of the most-listened-to radio station in the Rhein-Main area and will be among the first ones to know if Obersturmführer Ulbert shows up. I took the liberty of offering him a deal if he tips us off."

"What kind of deal?" Propov's rage was fading, but his tone stayed suspicious. He didn't like it when his subordinates took the initiative, but at the same time he was intelligent enough to know about the need for clandestine operations, false leads, and generous offers to possible informants. And Böhm was a big fish.

Vladi could *see* the wheels in Propov's head turning and waited a few seconds to give his boss time to adjust to the new information. Now he just had to make it look as if it had been Propov's idea all along.

"You taught me to explore all options when confronted with a difficult problem. When I ran into Böhm here in Wiesbaden, I remembered your advice and invited him for a chat among old comrades." Vladi didn't mention that Böhm had been less than cooperative. "I planted the idea that he might get off the hook if he proves a useful ally for us. And then I mentioned Ulbert."

"Well done." Propov obviously felt flattered.

"I found out more about the ridiculous airlift, too." Vladi recounted his day at the airbase. By the end of the conversation, his boss was quite pleased, although the information itself wasn't new, it was good to have it confirmed by another source.

"Well done. Nevertheless, I need you here for an urgent matter. Return to Berlin immediately! I'll have a car waiting for you in Marienborn."

"All right. I'll take the train to Helmstedt tomorrow and cross the border on foot. By the way, I'm traveling as Gerd Schmidt from Erfurt."

"The driver will be informed."

A click on the line indicated that Propov had ended the conversation, and Vladi let out a deep sigh. He'd feared some backlash for going it alone, but it had gone surprisingly well.

THE NEXT MORNING he got up early and walked to the train station, where he bought a ticket to Helmstedt. The train would leave around noon, and he decided to splurge his allowance on a breakfast in that café Böhm had taken him to. His mouth watered at the memory of those heavenly pastries.

The weather had cleared up and everything looked neat and tidy. Except for shining droplets on trees and bushes, nothing remained of the fluvial rains from the day before. Despite the sun lurking behind some clouds, it was chilly and none of the outdoor tables were occupied. He didn't mind and chose the seat from where he could overlook all other tables and watch the passers-by.

Biting into an especially fantastic-looking sweet pie called *Johannisbeerstreusel*, red currant streusel, he closed his eyes to relish the sweet and sour flavors exploding on his tongue, the mixture a revelation of confectionary art. It reminded him of the joy he'd felt as young boy when his mother had made *Smokwa*, a traditional Russian sweet made of plums, apples or other fruits boiled in honey or sugar syrup.

Those days were long gone. He shrugged. Thoughts of his mother always made him nostalgic, since she'd died in the Great Patriotic War. He opened his eyes again to take another bite, when he noticed two Americans, looking like they'd come straight from hell, settling at the table next to him and asking for extra strong coffee.

"After that horrendous day yesterday, I am not sure how long we can continue the airlift," the tall, slim one with dark hair and more stubble than was appropriate for a serviceman said.

"Did the old man say so?" the shorter, burly man answered.

"No, but he was out of his mind. You'd think he was about to strangle every last person in the tower for their failure to talk down the aircraft."

"You managed to land in time for this celebration."

The man shrugged. "Just barely. I can tell you I was covered in sweat from the moment we passed the Fulda beacon. If you ask me, that was the end of it. I have no idea how we are going to supply Berlin with coal once the cold season approaches."

Vladi all but gleamed with delight. Sokolov would be so very pleased to hear this. But already in the next moment he deflated again.

"Don't be such a doom-monger, Glenn. Nobody is willing to hand the bloody Soviets Berlin on a silver platter. This fight is not over yet."

Glenn sighed. "I really need to get some sleep after that hell of a night."

Vladi had heard enough and looked at his wristwatch. It was almost time to leave for the train station. He stood up to walk across the street and would have stepped in front of a jeep, had it not been for the quick reaction of Glenn, who jumped up and pushed him out of harm's way. Vladi fell to the ground and felt a stabbing pain to his knees and hands. The next moment he heard brakes and people jumping out of the jeep, agitatedly talking in English.

That was just what he needed. American military demanding his papers and asking him a myriad questions. They might even want to take him to one of their hospitals. What a great way to stay under the radar! So, he quickly scrambled to his feet, dusted off the dirt and raised his hands, saying loudly in German, *"Mir geht es gut. Nichts passiert."* Then he repeated the same sentence in English. "I'm good. Nothing happened."

He glanced at Glenn. "I'll be eternally grateful for your fast reflexes. You saved my life."

"Nothing to speak of."

Vladi quickly disappeared in the gathering crowd. It wouldn't do for the Americans to find out who he really was. Shortly thereafter, he arrived at the station and settled in the waiting room. The man next to him was reading a newspaper, and Vladi's gaze fell on the headline announcing a mineworkers ' strike in the Ruhr region.

That was a bizarre thing to do, since coal was so important for the German industry, so he murmured, "How on earth do the British even allow this?"

The newspaper owner heard him and looked over with an indignant expression. "Striking is a basic democratic right."

In theory that was true, but in the Soviet Union nobody ever went on strike, because that would only damage the industrial progress, which in turn would hurt the very people who went on strike. "Don't those miners see that they are only damaging themselves?"

"You are a funny guy, where are you from?"

"Berlin," said Vladi and realized in the same moment his mistake, because the eyes of his counterpart became wide.

"You do know that you can't return by train, right?"

"I do. I'm actually going to Hamburg where I'll stay with friends until the travel restrictions are lifted."

"Travel restrictions? Bloody inhumane blockade. The Russians are despicable louts!"

Vladi winced and longed to punch the man in the face, but thought better of it and gave him a surly smile. Thankfully his train arrived and he fled from the waiting hall to avoid further discussion.

During the long journey he had quite some time to reflect. Despite everything it had been a successful trip. He had two irons in the fire to find Obersturmführer Ulbert before the clueless brute Captain Grusow. His bets were on Werner Paulevich Böhm. Judging by the fear Vladi had seen in his eyes, Böhm was very motivated to contact him if he ever found out about Ulbert.

Very proud of himself and his latest move, Vladi closed his eyes, lulled to sleep be the monotonous rattle.

19

ZARA

Zara enjoyed working for the Gardners and without even noticing she put on some weight. While the food wasn't fancy or extravagant, there was always enough of it. The abundance in comparison to what she had experienced in Berlin left her feeling guilty for her friends who'd suffered even more shortages since the Soviets had begun the blockade.

Charles Gardner worked in the supply department at the Wiesbaden airbase and often mentioned things like tonnages, calories and basic needs. Like everyone else, he was worried that a bad weather spell similar to that horrific rainstorm a while ago might send the entire operation tumbling, and to feed the population after that they might have to concede to the Soviets.

Obviously, he never spoke those words out loud, but Zara guessed his worries from muffled arguments over the phone and sorrowful gazes. The Americans had set their minds on defying the Russians and staying in Berlin – at any price. But neither their powerful economy nor the millions of dollars behind their military machine could bargain with the weather, especially the awful November fog Berlin was famous for.

Zara was cooking dinner when the door opened and Mr. Gardner stepped inside with Glenn in tow. Whether she liked it or not, her stomach always filled with butterflies when she saw Glenn, and she had the suspicion that his frequent visits to the Gardner household weren't made exclusively to rekindle the old friendship with her employer.

"Hello, Zara." Glenn cast her that charming smile of his, and she felt a delicious prickle running along her skin.

"Hello," she said and turned toward Mr. Gardner. "I didn't know you were bringing a guest for dinner. I haven't…"

He interrupted her, "Don't worry, just put another plate on the table. I'm sure there'll be enough food."

"Shall I inform your wife? She's out with the children visiting a friend of hers, but I could call over the phone."

"No need. We'll be fine."

Zara wasn't sure she would be fine in Glenn's perturbing presence and hoped that she could sneak away as soon as possible.

"Dinner will be ready in ten minutes. Do you want me to serve it in the dining room?" Normally she ate together with the family at the table, but when Cath and the children weren't home, Mr. Gardner would usually eat alone in his study while she remained in the kitchen.

"Yes, please. And if you don't mind, please join us," Mr. Gardner said.

"Certainly." On purpose, she took the seat farthest away from Glenn and at an angle where she didn't have to look at him.

The men talked about global politics and the life back home in the States, and just when she thought they'd forgotten about her, Glenn said, "That food is the best I've ever eaten. Where did you learn to cook so well?"

She glowered at his thinly-veiled attempt to flirt with her. "In the *Bund Deutscher Mädel*." At least her rebuke kept him silent long enough until Cath returned with the children.

John and Lisa immediately jumped on Glenn and demanded he play with them, which he did. Zara served Cath the plate she'd reserved for her and secretly observed Glenn, who seemed to enjoy wrestling with two children. It was such a delight watching him that she felt guilty for her nasty answer. Not that he hadn't deserved it, because he simply wouldn't stop trying to hit on her.

In that very moment, he caught her staring at him and winked. She felt herself flush violently and dashed into the kitchen, afraid he might follow her and she wouldn't find the willpower to resist his charms. When he didn't, she was disappointed. Sometime later, Glenn wrestled the two children into bed and returned downstairs with an exhausted expression on his face.

"I have no idea how you manage to get them to sleep every day," he said to Zara.

She giggled. "The secret is to promise a bedtime story if they behave well."

His wonderful brown eyes sparkled with amusement. "That's all? A bedtime story? And you don't have to fight them every step of the process? You don't even have to threaten to knock out their teeth if they don't brush them?"

"You're hilarious." Zara laughed.

"Usually people tell me I'm reckless and irresponsible, so I take it as a compliment." His face was suddenly within inches of hers and she held her breath, fearing and hoping at once that he would kiss her. A delicate tension prickled between them, dragging out as neither of them dared to move.

"Zara, could you serve us whisky in the library, please?" Mr. Gardner's request destroyed the moment and rescued her from having to decide what to do if Glenn actually kissed her. Much to her chagrin, she felt a twinge of disappointment. "Yes. In a moment."

Glenn's face mirrored her own feelings. "I'm afraid our relationship is a succession of bad timings."

"I'm afraid we don't have a relationship."

"Definitely not my fault." He winked at her, before he turned around to join the Gardners in the library, which was the most beautiful room of the house. Zara always wondered to whom the villa had belonged before the American military had requisitioned it.

It must have been a lover of books, because the library was fully equipped from floor to ceiling with dark wooden bookshelves filled with big tomes of ancient books, German classics and modern literature. The library had a wealth of stories to choose from and a person could easily lose herself in there for days and weeks without ever having to emerge. The Gardners never read any of the books, probably because their German wasn't good enough, but Zara often borrowed one to read at night in her bed.

She served the Gardners and Glenn whisky and then retreated to the kitchen to clean the dishes. Through the open door she could hear them talk. Soon the discussion became more heated and turned toward the airlift. Zara perked up her ears, as their arguments were echoing her own thoughts. The weather was the big question mark behind the entire operation.

"We need to stock up a reserve store of coal or there's not a chance in hell we'll get through winter. But every single additional ton will have to be flown in at the expense of foodstuffs," Mr. Gardner said.

"Tonnage has gone up every day since General Tunner arrived," Glenn said.

"Yes, but since Black Friday we've had three days with less than one thousand tons."

"That will always happen, what is important is the week-over-week comparison, and that has increased."

"Both airports are at full capacity, there's no way to increase tonnage further to build up the reserves."

"We're building a new airport at Tegel."

Zara's head jerked around, since she hadn't known this. The Americans were actually building a new airport in the block-aded city? How on earth did they plan to accomplish this feat?

"The new airport won't solve the weather problem. During the worst flying season we'll need the most coal. Six thousand tons a day. And that's just for heating public buildings, hospitals and power plants. This doesn't even include heating for private households. How do you think Berliners will hold up if the winter is even remotely as harsh as it was two years ago?"

Six thousand tons? Only for coal? It was an unimaginable number. Next, Zara heard Mrs. Gardner's voice. "Don't do you think the Soviets will lift the blockade to avoid people freezing to death?"

Both men laughed at the same time and Mr. Gardner said, "I'll bet my ass these soulless monsters will see their bloody crime through to the bitter end."

"Charles, watch your language," Cath said.

But he only laughed. "The children are in bed."

Zara heard Glenn trying to calm the heated discussion. "They're counting on the Berliners to waver in their determination to hold up, and switch sides. If enough West Berliners register their ration cards in the East the Soviets will use it as one more reason to push us out, claiming the people have voted with their feet. And if — God forbid — the lord mayor should ask the Western Powers to cede our control over Berlin to the Soviets in the name of saving two million citizens from starvation, we can't very well refuse."

"Why do we even want to keep this island of rubbish instead of letting the Russians have it?" Cath asked.

"Oh, dear," her husband answered. "It's not just Berlin that is at stake. It's the hegemony over Germany and Europe, ultimately over the entire world. The Soviets will exploit every perceived weakness and if we don't put our foot down in Berlin, they will soon rule the world and enslave much of the population like they have the unfortunate nations behind the Iron Curtain."

Zara finished cleaning the kitchen. She dried her hands on her apron and hung it on the kitchen door, before she stepped into the library, asking, "Do you need anything else? Otherwise I will go to bed."

"No thank you, Zara, have a good night," Cath said.

Just as she walked out, Glenn got up and followed her. "Will you go out with me?"

"No."

"Why not?" He was blocking the staircase.

"Because you're annoying me. Now get out of my way."

"I remember making you laugh half an hour ago. Why do you resist going out with me? We would have so much fun. Promise." He looked at her with the cutest puppy eyes and despite her determination to stay terse, she had to laugh.

"See, I amuse you."

His smile was to die for, but she wouldn't let him know. "If I wanted to be amused I would go and watch a Charlie Chaplin movie."

"I can take you if you want."

For a moment she wavered. Why did he have to be so incredibly handsome and kind? "Thanks, but I think I'll pass."

"Will you let me know when you change your mind?"

"Don't count on it. And now, can you please step out of my way?"

He stepped aside, calling after her. "You're the most desirable woman I've ever met."

Zara rushed into her room and threw herself onto the bed. She needed the complication of a relationship with an Ami soldier like she needed a sore thumb.

20

GLENN

S everal weeks into General Tunner's command and every last member of Operation Vittles adored him. The conditions for the crews had vastly improved, because he managed the living conditions for his men in the same meticulous and efficient way he attended to air logistics.

The first thing he had done was to separate sleeping quarters according to the roster, so that the nightshift could come and go without waking up the dayshift. It was also an open secret that Tunner had engaged in a rather nasty argument with the guys from the ordinary Occupation Forces to arrange for more sleeping quarters, more showers, more kitchens, more of everything for the temporary airlift crews.

Instead of hopping onto an aircraft whenever he found one, Glenn checked the roster in the flight office and knew his schedule a week in advance. Operation Vittles had ceased to be a cowboy adventure and had become a standard military operation, where everyone worked according to a plan.

Glenn took a short detour to the canteen to stuff a quick breakfast into his mouth, because he was running late for the briefing. Downing a cup of coffee with one hand, he leafed through the newest issue of the Air Force newspaper, the *Daily Task Force*.

It was maybe the most ingenious of Tunner's innovations. A daily bulletin with the weather forecast, tonnages, and other important news. However, Glenn wasn't interested in any of this at the moment. He went straight to the page with the daily cartoon by the gifted Jake Schuffert.

As soon as he saw today's image, he all but spit out his coffee laughing. It was titled "Airlift Intrigue or How Records Are Broken" and showed twice the same picture of a comical man, dubbed Airlift efficiency expert, at his desk, a lit cigarette in his mouth. In the left image he was shouting into the radio receiver, "Hello, Celle, I hear Fassberg is way ahead of you on tonnage today," while on the right side he was repeating the same message, but this time addressing the Fassberg base.

The competition between the airbases was fierce and everyone wanted to be the base who lifted the most tonnage into Berlin on any given day, week, or month. It was another of the things Tunner had implemented and every week, the winning airbase received an award. It was all in good fun, despite the knowledge that the high brass was actively exploiting the common soldier's competitive spirit for the sake of efficiency.

He grabbed two donuts and rushed out the door. He had only two minutes left before the briefing started. The days of chaos were gone, and if Tunner hated one thing it was unpunctuality.

On his way another pilot, called Jim, fell into step with him. "Hey, Glenn, have you heard?"

"Heard what? You're rotated?"

Jim, who'd made no secret of the fact that he yearned to get home to his wife and children, grimaced. "Not yet. Still hoping. But there's this fellow. Gail Halvordsen. You know him?"

"The guy who is always out and about with his handheld movie camera?"

"Yep."

"What's he done?"

"You won't believe it. Time before last when he was in Tempelhof, he noticed about two dozen children crowded behind the barbed-wire fence around the airfield."

To watch the aircraft land and take off was one of the main attractions for the Berlin children. Every day Glenn saw them huddling near the fence, looking into the sky and shouting above each other about who had first identified the type of the plane coming in. He grinned. What kid worth its salt didn't love plane-spotting?

Back in the days when the crews had been allowed to leave the airfield, he'd often come across groups of children begging for something, usually chocolate or chewing gum.

"He gave them gum?" Glenn asked.

Jim was Halvordsen's co-pilot, and seemed eager to show off his first-hand information. "He did, but he only had two sticks for them to share. And now here's the thing: On the flight home he told me that he promised the children to bring in enough for everyone and he'd drop the candy from his plane. And the next time, we did."

"Drop candy? Wouldn't they get hurt if they accidentally got hit?" They had reached the administration building and rushed up the stairs, taking two steps at once.

"Parachutes."

Glenn jerked his head around, looking at Jim as if he had a screw loose. Jim, though, beamed all over and nodded at the door to the flight office. "I'll tell all about it after the briefing."

Fifteen minutes later the meeting ended, and Glenn sidled up to Jim to ask, "You were kidding me, right? There's no way to parachute candy."

Jim beckoned at some other men to come over. "Here's the

thing. Gail promised the children to drop candy for all of them, and to wiggle his wings approaching Tempelhof, so they would know it was him."

Glenn raised his eyebrow. It was a great idea, and he could only imagine how much the kids would love this. But he was still concerned about dropping stuff out of the aircraft. "Weren't you afraid of injuring the kids?"

"We were. That's why we made parachutes out of our hand-kerchiefs and tied them to the candy. It worked like a charm. You can't imagine how heartwarming it was to see the group of children eagerly waiting for us," Jim said with a nostalgic voice, clearly missing his own children. "Bob, our flight engineer, opened the window and pushed the candy parachutes out. They safely floated to the ground and by the time we had landed we saw the children next to the fence grinning and sharing the treats, waving to all of us."

"It was probably the best thing that happened to them in months," Glenn said.

"Yep, right?" Jim beamed from ear to ear, before he started his frontal attack on the men present. "We are collecting candy rations. Would you be willing to donate yours to our cause?"

Glenn hadn't seen this coming, but he didn't need long to consider and readily agreed, "Sure. I'll find you later and bring you my chocolates."

"Do you even have permission to do this? I mean we can't simply throw things out of our aircraft," one of the older men said.

Jim flinched. "By the time we get permission, the airlift will be over."

Throughout the day, Glenn told everyone he met about the project and collected the chocolate rations most of his fellow airmen eagerly handed over. At night he made little parachutes with his crew, tied the collected candy to them and then searched for Jim and Gail to give them the results of a day's work.

"Wow, thanks, man, that's awesome. Where did you get all these chocolates?"

Throughout the next weeks Gail, once a week, dropped the candy supplies collected by the airmen. Glenn and several others spent a good deal of their leisure time making parachutes and tying them to the sweets.

It was a welcome distraction to keep his thoughts off Zara, because he was at his wits' end where she was concerned. Every time they met he could sense her attraction to him, but she always rebuffed his advances.

Maybe it was time to call it quits and pursue a more willing Fräulein, since there was no shortage of German girls eager to go out with an American soldier. He decided to give it one more shot and if she still showed him the cold shoulder, he would leave her alone.

"Did you see the crowd of children this morning?" one of his companions asked.

"Unbelievable, isn't it?"

"I've been told they're waiting for hours until Uncle Wiggly comes in."

"That's what they call him?"

"Yep. Uncle Wiggly in his *Rosinenbomber*. That's their word for candy bomber."

The door opened and a young soldier Glenn didn't know stepped inside. "Captain Davidson?"

"Yes, what's up?"

"General Tunner wants to see you."

Glenn grimaced and wondered what the old man could want from him. He hurried to the administration building and met Jim and Gail in the corridor, headed for the same destination.

He eyed them suspiciously. "Do you know what this is all about?"

"It's about the candy bombers," Jim said with a sad face.

"If he's going to court-martial us, I'll tell him it was all my idea," Gail offered.

Court-martial? Glenn swallowed. He was known to be reckless and care little about rules and regulations, but he'd never done anything that would warrant being court-martialed. He hoped his military career wouldn't end because he'd helped an honorable mission. Judging by the faces of the two other men, they had the same queasy stomach awaiting the inevitable.

Tunner's face was unreadable when he finally asked them inside and said, "Whose idea was it to drop the candy?"

Gail stepped forward. "Mine, sir. These two guys have nothing to do with it."

Tunner unexpectedly broke out into a chuckle. "Not to worry. You're on to something here. It's a great idea and we should use it for propaganda purposes."

A heavy burden fell from Glenn's shoulders and by the looks of it, his two friends felt the same way. Nobody spoke until Tunner raised his voice again, "We'll make this an official operation and I'll even designate a man to organize it. With proper support we can ask for candy and handkerchief donations not only among the soldiers on base, but also with the German population in our zone and with the people back home in the States."

Glenn was completely dumbfounded and had one more reason to admire his commander. On September 22 the operation was officially announced in the *Daily Task Force* as Operation Little Vittles and soon they couldn't keep up with the amount of candy donated and shipped across the Atlantic.

The dropping was done by any pilot who agreed to it. It was a slightly tricky task, since they couldn't just open the cockpit door during the flight. Instead one of the crew members had to use the emergency dropping shaft behind the pilot's seat that all Skymasters had and that could be opened mid-air to drop the little parachutes.

On one of those flights, Glenn was approaching Tempelhof when the aircraft in front of him was blown out of the landing strip and had to go round. Since he was the next in line he mentally prepared himself to be sent to a waiting circle while the other pilot got a second try.

"Big Easy Four," came the voice from ground control. "Circle out of the airport space and return home. Big Easy Five, begin your landing approach."

"Hey, you sleeping? That's us!" Glenn's co-pilot shouted.

"Us what?"

"Landing now. Have you forgotten there's no more waiting circles?"

Indeed he had. Shortly after that fateful Black Friday a rule had been put in place to abolish the dangerous waiting circles over the city. Whenever a machine couldn't land at the first attempt, it had to return back to its home base fully loaded.

Glenn was maybe ten seconds late and pondered whether it was still safe to land or whether he should go around. Normally he didn't care that much about a soft landing, but his Skymaster was filled to the brim with precious black diamonds, as they had dubbed the coal, because each piece was more costly than a real diamond after flying it into Berlin. He sure as hell didn't want a rough landing with the possibility of a coal dust explosion shattering the aircraft and the crew to smithereens.

"Not sleeping. Going down now. Take out the landing gear."

He touched down soft as a feather with extra space to go on the landing strip and taxied his Skymaster to the unloading positions, where a crew of eager German workers unloaded the entire cargo of ten tons in only thirteen minutes, which gave him and the rest of the crew barely enough time to grab a snack and a cup of strong, hot coffee.

Leaving the cockpit, Glenn stretched his legs and walked over to the mobile snack bar parked on the airfield. It was another innovation, helping the crew to stay close to their planes and making the most of their short stay, before returning home.

"Hello, sweetheart, coffee please, hot and strong," he greeted the beautiful blonde German girl working in the snack bar. Every day he and his fellows thanked the recruiter who'd had the foresight to employ only the best looking Fräuleins for the job. A welcome sight for sore eyes after many hours of flight duty.

This particular one was called Helga and she always greeted the airmen with a huge smile, good-naturedly going along with their attempts to flirt with her. The airmen weren't allowed to stay in Berlin, but had to return home right away, so there was no harm in the coffee ladies pretending they might be up for a tryst.

"I know a bar in Wiesbaden with knockout girls," Teddy said, biting into a donut.

Much to his own surprise, Glenn shook his head. Zara still floated around in his head and he wasn't interested in anyone else, which was a first for him. Less than ten minutes later the German workers had unloaded the plane, and another work crew jumped inside the cargo department to sweep out the dangerous coal dust, accumulating in every crook and cranny, regardless of how carefully the coal was wrapped in the army issue kitbags.

"All ready, sir," a member of the ground crew overseeing the unloading told Glenn, who thanked him and walked over to the mobile weather station, where they handed him a sheet of paper with his takeoff slot and weather forecast along the route, which was updated regularly with the information the pilots in the air reported to the tower. Operation Vittles truly had become a conveyor belt.

"Bye, Helga, it was a delight, like always," Glenn said before he and his crew made to board the aircraft again. Helga rewarded him with one of her brightest smiles, but for some strange reason he compared it to Zara's smile and it faded. Not that Zara had ever bestowed one of her heartwarming smiles on him, but he had seen them on her face playing with the Gardner children. He was sure it would knock his socks off once she actually aimed one at him.

Back in the cockpit, Teddy joked, "For three months, we've been coming every day to have our coffee break in Berlin. The guys at home would be so jealous about our fanciness."

21

ZARA

C ath came home and called out, "Zara. Where are you?"

Zara wiped her hands on her apron and walked out of the kitchen. "In the kitchen preparing dinner."

"This is so exciting!" Cath waved an issue of the *Daily Task Force* in her hand and showed it to Zara. "They are asking for donations of handkerchiefs and candies for the children in Berlin."

Zara took the news bulletin and read the short article about Operation Little Vittles. "What a nice thing to do." Her mind wandered back to Berlin with all the undernourished and stick-thin children who barely scraped by even before the blockade. She shivered at the notion of how much worse the situation must have gotten. It would do them good to catch some candy dropping from the planes, if only to reassure them the world had not forgotten about them.

Herself, she lived in a rosy bubble with the Gardner family, who, as members of the occupation forces, never endured shortages. She longed to see her friends and make sure they were okay, but visits weren't possible for civilians and their communication relied solely on the rare letters. Twice she had sent them a small care package with food and money through Mr. Gardner's connections.

"I have been asked to organize the effort here at the base." Cath was very active in several military wives' circles and charities, therefore it didn't come as a complete surprise, although her next words knocked the breath from Zara's lungs. "I thought you could help me with the German population. Do you think they would donate?"

Zara furrowed her brow, thinking. Three years after the downfall, the Germans in the Bizone still struggled with the devastation the war had left behind, but compared to the people in Berlin they were incredibly well off. While some might object, she was sure most families would gladly donate if not candy then at least handkerchiefs for the starving children in the besieged city.

Once again, unadulterated hate for the Soviets attacked her and threatened to explode her heart. How on earth could they believe it was a good idea to starve more than two million by blocking off any and all supply routes to them?

Despite Vladi's explanations that this wasn't a blockade, but merely a form of traffic control and that no one was trying to starve civilians, she would scratch his eyes out if he were standing in front of her right now. The whole excuse that Berliners could go and register their ration cards in the East was a big, fat trap that would only lead to more oppression and enslavement under the communist thumb.

Gratefully the vast majority of Berliners saw through the propaganda of thinly-veiled lies and blatant misinterpretations of the SED press and would rather suffer from hunger than give up their freedom for all eternity.

She pitied the people in the Soviet occupied zone who didn't have the luxury of choice and had to live under the brutal communist regime, whether they believed in it or not.

"And? Do you think they will donate?" Cath asked once again.

"I think it's a fantastic idea, and I'm sure we can convince the people in Wiesbaden to gift something for the children. Just how do we reach them? It's not like we can go from door to door and knock everywhere like the carol singers."

Cath gave a confused look and Zara explained, "The carol singers are a German tradition. They represent the three Wise Men and knock on doors on January 6th, to bestow a blessing on the household in exchange for a small gift, usually a few pennies or food."

"I'm not going to sing," Cath protested with a laugh. "And you're right, it's not practical to go from house to house, especially since the people are so mistrustful."

"We need to go places where many people gather," Zara said.

"What if we put out flyers at the ration card office? Every household has to go there once a week and they'll know it's approved by the military administration if they find it there."

"But a mere flyer might not have the desired impact. You know how people either don't pick up the flyers or don't read them. Even if they read them, they might go home and forget."

Cath shook her head, her brown hair bouncing off her shoulders. "Right. We need an instant commitment. People who will drive the cause and help us convince others."

"Germans who are well liked in the community," Zara said. The population had slowly grown to like the Americans and saw them less as the occupier and more as friends, but to pluck at people's heartstrings, the cause would need to come from within.

"You might be right. It's always better if these kinds of things aren't imposed by the government. How about teachers?"

It took Zara a few seconds to understand where Cath was

going, but then she nodded. "That's perfect. We could first talk to the teachers, and then prepare a speech to hold in the class-rooms and ask the children to donate for their counterparts in Berlin. I'm sure they would love to help."

"We could make it a competition between different classes."

Zara had to smile. That was so typical American. They had to make a competition out of everything.

"Yes, I think that could work. Do we need some official permission to do this?"

Cath beamed with excited energy. "I already have all the official permissions I need to contact whomever I want to in order to organize donations for Operation Little Vittles."

They spent the remainder of the day making leaflets to distribute and making lists of teachers to approach.

22

VLADI

As usual, General Sokolov was livid. He'd called for a meeting in the SMAD headquarters and stood at the head of the table droning on with vicious accusations against the Americans.

"This is unacceptable." Sokolov yelled, before taking a pregnant pause.

Vladi involuntarily sat straighter and perked up his ears. Everything the Americans, and especially Sokolov's nemesis, General Harris, said or did was unacceptable to begin with, so he wondered what it was this time.

Looking at Sokolov it must be something extreme, because his face was redder than usual and even from his place at the other end of the table, Vladi noticed the pulsating vein on the general's temple.

"My medicine," Sokolov hissed angrily at his secretary, trying to hide how much his ulcers troubled him. If the ulcers didn't do him in, a heart attack would surely do, if the old man continued with those violent fits of rage.

But until that day Vladi would patiently stand at attention and endure the verbal abuse that reminded him of his teacher at school, with the difference that his teacher had emphasized the words with a stick. Vladi had been the recipient of such a scolding many, many times. Even now, his backside hurt from remembering those times.

Beside him, Colonel Ulyanin, the Air Forces commander, and several party functionaries were attending the meeting. Nobody dared utter a word, because they all knew that when Sokolov was raging, a single wrong word could send a man to Siberia.

"This is another manifestation of the atrocious corruption that signifies the American way of life. But never in my wildest dreams would I have believed they could stoop this low. Not even Hitler's fascists, whom we've been fighting for more than a decade, were capable of such inhumanities." Sokolov paused for breath, his face a pained grimace. "The imperialist devils have shown their true colors, and it turns out, they're worse than the fascists. In fact, they are the new fascists and we have to fight them with everything we've got. Not only for the great Soviet nation, but also for the innocent souls in Germany and the rest of our brother countries."

Vladi's interest was piqued. What horrible thing had the Americans done this time?

"Corrupting innocent children with chocolates!"

Vladi had to bite on his lip to keep himself from laughing out loud at this utterly ridiculous statement. Sokolov had decided to make the *Rosinenbomber* and their candy parachutes a topic of vital importance. Operation Little Vittles was less than a week old and, as he'd expected, Moscow was concerned about the public image the Americans had created with their gesture of generosity.

It was nothing less than a propaganda disaster. What kid didn't like candy? Vladi suspected the bosses were so pissed off about this harmless endeavor, because they wanted candy, too, but he quickly pushed these heretical thoughts aside and made a sorrowful-stern face, nodding at every horrible accusation Sokolov launched against the devilish Americans.

After ten minutes of the general's yelling, screaming, and slamming his fists onto the oak desk with such force that the floor shook, Vladi himself was convinced that chocolates were the root of all evil and needed to be eradicated from the face of the earth — along with Capitalism and Industrialism.

During a short pause, Sokolov's secretary peeked into the room looking like a frightened mouse, holding the anti-ulcer medicine like a shield in front of her.

Sokolov grabbed the liquid, emptied the entire glass in one big gulp and glared at each man in the audience, one after another. When it was Vladi's turn, it made him feel as if the oxygen were being sucked from his lungs.

"I want this to stop! Make it stop!" Sokolov pointed directly at poor Colonel Ulyanin and everyone else in the room seemed to sigh with relief.

"Comrade General, if I may speak?" Ulyanin said in a subdued voice.

"You may!" Daggers flew from Sokolov's eyes and Vladi wouldn't want to be in Ulyanin's shoes. "We're going into October and soon the skies over Berlin will be full of fog, making it impossible to land."

"Is this all you have got? Hoping for General Winter to save us? Don't you think your department could be doing a little bit more? Shoot the Americans out of the sky!"

The rather short and stocky man with black hair and a big mustache modeled after Stalin's seemed to shrink even more under the slew of insults Sokolov hurled at him. Ulyanin really wasn't to be envied, since he couldn't please his boss and shoot down their allies' planes.

"Comrade General, as much as I agree with you and your superior wisdom, my hands are bound by diplomatic procedures in this case. Don't get me wrong, I personally think it's a fantastic idea and I would be willing to do it in the blink of an eye, but if we shoot down an American aircraft, there will be repercussions. Stalin himself said our great nation is not ready for another war."

Sokolov's red face turned a shade of deep purple and his eyes bulged out of their sockets, ready to pop out at any second. Ulyanin hastily added, "Not yet at least. We will be ready when the time comes and thanks to Comrade Stalin's great foresight we will be victorious again."

Vladi sincerely doubted that. After all, the Americans had the atomic bomb, while the Soviets didn't. The misanthropic thugs hadn't hesitated to use the bomb against the Japanese and would drop one on Moscow with the same glee.

Until the great Soviet Union had their own atomic bomb, they would have to stay low and endure whatever insults the imperialist world hurled at them.

"Do something! And do it now!" Sokolov burst out, spittle flying from his mouth.

"Of course, Comrade General," Ulyanin said and shone with relief when Sokolov dismissed them.

Once they had left the office, Ulyanin approached Vladi. "Comrade Rublev, may I have a word?"

Vladi's first reaction was to tell the Colonel to bugger off, since this was a task where everyone involved could only lose. He was already on Sokolov's bad side, because the Americans had started constructing a third airport in Berlin, and the general had somehow decided it was Red Army Intelligence's fault.

But having the Colonel as an enemy would only make things worse, and perhaps they could help each other out by blaming things on another department, the NKVD coming first to his mind.

"We've been buzzing American aircraft consistently in the corridor. It's highly dangerous and we've had many close calls.

Just last week one of my best fighters died in an accident. I have no idea what else to do short of actually shooting them out of the sky, which we both know is not an option."

Vladi rubbed a hand across his jaw. "What do you suggest?"

Ulyanin's face contorted with pain. "I swear I will end up with Sokolov's ulcers if this airlift lasts much longer. The experts agreed that the Americans can't provide an entire city from the air. But once again those stubborn bastards have shown us they defy logic and reason. Who would have believed they would drag aircraft from all over the world into Germany, just to keep two million fascists alive?"

"They certainly don't do it out of the goodness of their hearts. It's a ploy to win over the German population as friends in a desperate attempt to purloin what is ours. Their end goal is world domination." Even as he said it, Vladi wondered whether the American strategy to offer friendship wasn't much more successful than the Soviet way of intimidation and hardship.

"Yes, yes, but what can we do about it? It's not like we can suddenly act kindly toward the Germans. It would undermine our position and they'd stop respecting our authority."

Vladi had thought the same throughout most of his life-time, but with Zara he had witnessed that threats and even torture could only go so far. Instead, a bit of kindness often loosened tongues and sometimes resulted in loyal friends for life. Not that he considered Zara a friend, far from it. But she owed him and he was sure that one day she'd pay back the favor. If she didn't by handing over her father, another opportu-nity would show up.

People always paid the favors they owed. It was part of the human psychology and worked even in the Soviet system where the citizens had ingrained a fear of authority and a mistrust of friendship for decades.

"Increase activity in the air corridors. Make their lives

miserable and wait for General Winter to come to your aid. Then you can claim the success for yourself."

"What if this year the cold season doesn't bring fog and rain?"

"It will, Comrade Ulyanin, it will. People might not be reliable but nature always is." Vladi said confidently. "Fog and rain will sweep those pesky aircraft and their candy parachutes from the Berlin skies."

23

ZARA

Zara was so occupied with helping Cath to ask for candy donations, she had barely time to breathe. Throughout the day she visited schools, ration card offices, and sports events in addition to her household duties, and in the evening she and Cath sat down to organize the activities of the next day. Then she fell into bed and slept like a stone.

It was a pleasurable exhaustion, though, because she felt like she was actually doing something useful in her life. Helping children even with the symbolic act of a single candy bar felt so much better than embroidering pillows with the swastika, or asking for donations for the war effort.

She had come a long way and was grateful for the opportunity the Gardners had given her. She didn't miss her cold-hearted mother and her Nazi father in the least. On the contrary, whenever thoughts of him entered her mind, she pushed them away in a hurry, afraid that thinking of him might somehow conjure him up and he would stomp into her life and ruin her newfound happiness.

Never before had she realized that while not exactly

unhappy during her teenage years, she'd been completely externally controlled and none of the things she had learned or done had been of her own volition.

Even today she had no idea what she wanted to do with her life. As much as she enjoyed working for the Gardners, she didn't see herself becoming old as a housemaid and nanny. And she certainly didn't entertain the idea of becoming a housewife and mother like her own mother had been and in the way Hitler had envisioned life for every good German girl.

The next day, after collecting the donations of a school class, she carried the heavy bag straight to the airbase. Usually a young soldier who worked in the logistics department would meet her at the entrance gate and take her bag of candies to deliver directly to the flight office, where the pilots would pick up their share before boarding their planes.

But today he was nowhere to be found.

Zara loathed the idea of lugging the heavy bag home and returning in the morning. "Isn't there someone else who can receive this bag from me?"

She pleaded with the guard, who shook his head. "Orders are orders. I can't just give this bag to anyone. It must be Sergeant Miller or one of the pilots spearheading the operation."

Zara groaned. These military people didn't have the slightest flexibility. Reluctantly, she heaved the bag onto her shoulder and made to leave. Just as she turned around, she heard a familiar voice saying, "Hey, Zara, can I help you with this?"

Of course, the overly-confident, always-flirting Glenn had to show up. She sometimes suspected him of following her, because he accidentally appeared wherever she was - although she hadn't seen much of him lately, since she'd been so busy with Little Vittles. Despite her determination not to encourage him, she cast him a thankful smile, and in turn his eyes lit up with genuine delight. He really wasn't a bad guy. In fact, he was handsome, kind, funny, a bit reckless and always up for mischief. Life with him would certainly never be boring.

She inwardly shook her head at the train her thoughts had taken and then decided to give him the opportunity to behave like a proper gentleman and carry that sack to the Gardners.

"Actually, I wanted to leave this here, but the person in charge is not to be found."

"What is it?" Glenn pointed at the bag.

"Uhmmm, candy." For no reason at all Zara felt the heat rising to her cheeks.

"I'll take it," he said, sending her one of his incredible smiles.

With her head suddenly mushy enough to match her wobbly knees, she managed to say, "They are for the children. In Berlin, you know? The candy bombers?" She'd started blabbing. Everyone involved in the airlift knew about this. He must think her a complete idiot, which only aggravated her embarrassment. She clamped her mouth shut.

"Who doesn't know about Little Vittles?" Glenn grabbed the bag, accidentally touching her hand. An electric charge ran from her fingers all the way down to her toes.

She glanced toward the guard and shook her head. "I can't give it to you. I can only give it to Sergeant Miller or one of the pilots spearheading the operation."

Despite the disquieting sensation of having his hand so close to hers, she grabbed the bag tighter. An instant humming coursed through her body, distracting her from what he was saying.

"Zara?"

"Yes?"

"Did you hear what I said?"

"No." She wanted to run away from the emotions the gaze of his brown eyes evoked in her.

"The man in charge is standing right in front of you."

"You're not Sergeant Miller," she said, sounding dumb even to her own ears.

He chuckled. "You're right, I'm not. I'm much better-looking." Everything about him twinkled with mischief.

"You're not."

"Do you mean I am not him or I am not better-looking than him?"

It was clear what he wanted her to answer. She shook her head in despair. Glenn was incorrigible and she certainly wouldn't engage in friendly banter with him, as that would only encourage him to continue his very unwelcome flirting. Although that irresistible grin made her insides go weak and she seriously considered dropping the bag and flinging herself at him.

At the last moment she composed herself, clutching the bag like a sheet anchor. First of all, she wasn't in the least interested in him, and secondly, he probably practiced *the smile* with all the girls he met. She refused to become another notch in the belt of an American pilot.

"I'd better go," she said helplessly.

"Please, Zara. I'm one of the pilots spearheading the operation, and you can give the bag to me. Your candies are safe with me."

Naturally, he hadn't been able to resist making a saucy remark. She pursed her lips, putting on her best scolding-nanny face that always brought the Gardner children to reason. "How do I know this isn't one of your ruses?"

His face contorted as if she'd stabbed him and he put a hand in a dramatic gesture across his heart. "What have I done to deserve your poor opinion of me?"

Shame crept up Zara's neck and she knew her face would be flushed within seconds. It wasn't his fault that she was too attracted to him for her own good. "I'm sorry. You haven't done anything."

A leaden silence hung between them and she stepped from one foot to the other, pondering how to get this awkward situation back on track.

Glenn was the first one to speak up. "Why don't you ask the guard? He'll tell you that it's perfectly okay to give me the candy bag."

Zara cocked her head in dismay that she hadn't thought of this herself. If Glenn spoke the truth, the guard would verify it. "All right."

"May I?" he asked and after awaiting her nod, took the bag from her hands, hefting it over his shoulder. "Whoa! That's heavy! How did you even manage to lug it all the way here?" He glanced with admiration at her lithe figure.

Zara laughed. Most people underestimated her, because she was so skinny and soft-spoken – a secret she certainly wouldn't let him in on. Together they walked the short distance to the entrance gate and Glenn told the guard, "Sergeant, I am here to take the candy for Operation Little Vittles to the flight office."

The man looked up, somewhat surprised, but then nodded, "Of course, Captain Davidson."

Glenn turned around to Zara and asked, "Do you need a receipt?"

She nodded, surprised at his thoughtfulness. Apparently, he was a mischief-maker only in his leisure time. This small episode had given her a completely new view and appreciation for him.

"Will you wait for me, please? I'll just bring this to the flight office. I was on my way for lunch. May I invite you?"

After his being so friendly and saving her from dragging the heavy bag to the Gardner villa, she didn't have the heart to brush him off, and nodded.

As promised Glenn returned within five minutes, beaming like a schoolboy when he saw that she was waiting for him. "I'm so glad you're still here. I was afraid you would run away on me."

Zara's eyes widened in shock. Her English had become quite proficient during the past months, but she must have misunderstood him. He couldn't actually expect her to run away and marry him. They hadn't even gone on a first date. "I certainly won't!" She turned on her heel, about to rush off, when she felt his big hand on her shoulder that nudged her to turn around.

"What happened? What did I say wrong?" He seemed truly concerned.

"Wrong? You expect me to run away and marry you and now you ask what you said wrong?"

"Oh... I'm so sorry. I only meant that I was afraid you might run away from here while I was dropping off the bag of candies."

"Oh..." Zara felt utterly stupid and would have darted off if it weren't for his hand on her shoulder.

"Will you still go out for lunch with me?"

As if to answer his question her stomach rumbled loudly.

"Can I take that as a yes?" he asked and she nodded.

24

GLENN

Glenn was in the shower room, smearing brilliantine into his unruly hair. But try as he might, it simply refused to stay back in the slick, fashionable look so many of his pals wore. One of the mechanics strolled inside, covered from top to toe in motor oil.

"Nice look, David," Glenn couldn't help but laugh, although the poor guy had probably spent the better part of his day beneath a leaking aircraft.

David scowled at him, before his glance fell on the jar of brilliantine and a lazy grin spread on his lips. "Going on a date?"

"Nothing special..." Glenn wouldn't admit that he was more nervous than when he'd asked big-breasted Suzie to go out with him as a junior in high school.

"Has to be pretty special. I've never seen you trying to put that slick stuff in your hair."

"It doesn't work, my hair is just too unruly," Glenn said with a defeated tone and didn't notice how David approached him. He was so preoccupied with looking his best for taking out Zara tonight. After that first lunch date two weeks earlier, they'd been seeing each other on a regular basis and he still couldn't believe his luck.

She was not only lithe and beautiful, but also intelligent and a good conversation partner. Sure, she had all these strange notions acquired in her Nazi childhood, but apart from that she was funny, sexy, interesting…and tonight he would finally give her a real kiss. One that would make her see stars and pave the way for more. Because, much to his dismay, all she'd allowed him so far was a quick peck on her lips to say goodnight.

Suddenly David stood beside him, interrupting his daydreams with an evil smirk on his face. "You need the good stuff." The next moment his greasy hands were all over Glenn's head rubbing motor oil into his hair.

"See how well it works?" David doubled over with laughter and after one glance in the mirror at the disaster that now sat on his head, Glenn jumped at the other man. Seconds later, they were rolling on the floor in a fistfight, leaving black smear marks all over the white tiles, until the door opened and the commanding officer stepped in. Glenn and David scrambled to their feet, their glances pinned to their toes.

"What is going on here?" the officer bristled.

"Sorry, sir." There was nothing else Glenn could say to excuse their actions. They'd gone at each other's throats like schoolboys with too much testosterone roaming in their veins.

"I want to see both of you in my office in thirty minutes."

Glenn bit on his lip to stop himself crying out with frustration. In one hour, he was supposed to pick up Zara. "Yes, sir!" As soon as the officer had left the room and closed the door behind him, Glenn glared at David. "Nice job."

"You started it."

Glenn turned around and undressed to take another shower and scrub the motor oil from his skin and hair. At least he'd been in his fatigues and not the dress uniform, which waited freshly laundered in his locker.

There was no use moaning, so he hurried to get himself into presentable shape again and discarded the idea of combing his hair back in the slick style that was all the rage. Disgruntled, he rubbed himself dry and walked to his quarters with the dirty fatigues over his arm.

Zara would surely give him a hard time for showing up late. Today of all days! He'd wanted to look his best, because he had arranged two tickets for a concert held for the American troops and their families off-base that night.

In his dress uniform, but with humidity-frizzled hair, he made it just in time to the CO's office, where he almost ran into David, who came rushing from the opposite side of the hallway.

Luckily, the officer made it short and didn't ground them for the night. A heavy burden fell from Glenn's shoulders and he stormed out of the barracks to rush to the Gardners' house.

25

ZARA

With every passing minute Zara became angrier. She paced the room, looking at the clock for the umpteenth time, but no bell rang. Glenn should have picked her up fifteen minutes ago. Today of all days he had to be late!

She was so excited, looking forward to the concert with the crooner Andy Williams, whom she'd heard on radio and seen pictures of in the magazines Mrs. Gardner received from the States. He looked devastating with his slicked-back black hair, and his voice was to die for. She smiled and cast another glance first at the clock and then at the small mirror hanging on the opposite wall.

She'd taken extra care with her looks, putting on red lipstick and rolling her waist-long hair into elaborate waves pinned to her head. While she rhapsodized over Andy Williams, in real life she preferred a more down-to-earth man. Someone with rougher edges, looking slightly rugged and unkempt, always ready to go up against the rules and have some fun.

Having spent most of her youth with slick and streamlined

boys, she appreciated someone who didn't blindly believe everything he was told and had no qualms about thinking for himself. Someone like Glenn, who seemed not to have a care in the world, but nevertheless had his heart in the right place.

She shook her head, aghast at her own thoughts. Despite having grown to like him more by the day and enjoying his company immensely, she certainly wasn't in love with him. He was a nice distraction, nothing more. If she ever found herself a man, it wouldn't be an American soldier who could be rotated somewhere at any given time, never to be seen or heard of again.

When Glenn finally arrived, almost forty minutes late, she opened the door with a scowl, ready to scratch out his eyes.

"I'm so sorry," he said slightly breathless.

It was the first time she'd seen him in his dress uniform adorned with a multitude of decorations. He looked simply irresistible, especially because the impeccable uniform didn't match at all his tousled hair. When he conjured forth a bouquet of flowers from behind his back, she melted to a puddle at his feet. Maybe, just maybe, she would forgive him for being late.

Despite wanting to wrap her arms around him for looking so utterly cute with the guilty expression on his face, she kept a stern face. "Thank you, but you're late."

"I know." His face clearly showed his discomfort, but to give him credit, he owned up to his fault and said, "I got into a fight in the shower room."

"You what?" Zara was never quite sure when to take him seriously and when he was joking.

"Yes, we rolled on the ground like rowdy schoolboys and that pig messed me up from head to toe with motor oil. Chalk it up to my lucky stars, the CO appeared, I almost got grounded and the boss let me go only because I told him I had a beautiful woman waiting for me."

Now she was pretty sure he was pulling her leg. This story was too far-fetched to be true.

"Well, that's quite the excuse," she said, half laughing.

"You don't believe me?" He gave her the pleading puppy eyes that always weakened her resolve, and pressed a hand across his heart. "Every single word is true. You can ask my commanding officer."

"Really?" She wavered and opted for taking the bouquet from his hands. It was a dream of beautiful yellow roses, orange gardenias and red camellias. The scent wafted into her nose. What a thoughtful gesture.

"They are beautiful. I'd better get a vase for them." She quickly retreated, locating a vase in the kitchen and bringing the flowers upstairs to her room, where she sniffed at them again, unwelcome feelings of tenderness and attachment attacking her and making her jump backwards.

It wasn't the fault of the flowers or Glenn's fault either, but she wasn't ready to take this relationship into more serious waters. She didn't even know why, because Glenn had every-thing she wanted in a man, but a stubborn voice in her head kept telling her it was better not to get involved with anyone.

If only she could talk to her friends Marlene and Bruni to set her head straight and tell her what to do. A slight smile appeared on her lips, because she knew exactly what they would say.

"You don't need a man to take care of you, you're better off by yourself," Bruni, the vivacious and independent singer, would say.

"She doesn't need a man to maintain her, but love is so much more than that. I would say go for it," Marlene would say.

"Yes, go for it. Have all the fun you want, and make sure he showers you with gifts and attention. But don't fall in love."

"But falling in love is the whole point!" Marlene would protest.

Then they would continue talking over her head as if she weren't in the room, each one of them making her point about men in general and relationships in particular very clear, until Zara lost her patience and interrupted them, saying it had been a mistake to ask them for advice, if all they were doing was ignoring her.

Next, the three of them would start laughing, and Bruni would renew their friendship by opening a bottle of red wine that she always seemed to have in store, no matter how bad the rationing, since Bruni never seemed to be affected by the realities other people had to deal with.

"Are you alright?" Glenn called from downstairs.

She shrugged off the memories and yelled, "Coming." She stormed down into the living room, where he was waiting. It was her day off today, and her employers had already left for the same concert, while the children spent the night with friends of the family.

"Sorry," she hissed as she came to a skidding halt inches away from him, because he'd moved from the living room into the hallway, directly into her path.

As was to be expected he took advantage of the situation and wrapped his arms around her, pretending to keep her from stumbling. She couldn't help but feel the comfort and the warmth pouring over her like a hot shower after a long and cold day outside.

"What a stormy young lady." He put her on her own feet again before giving her a once-over and letting out a low whistle. "You look smashing."

Zara instinctively backed away from him, because she hated her good looks. Unlike her friend Bruni, she'd never learned to use them to her advantage and they had brought nothing but trouble throughout her adolescence. Every man she met seemed only interested in her pretty face, long legs and hourglass figure.

"I'm sorry, what did I say now?" Glenn seemed honestly confused, making her feel guilty. It wasn't his fault that she'd been exploited all her life.

"Nothing."

"It must be something, or you wouldn't make a face like three days of rain."

Despite her embarrassment she had to laugh at the way he used the German saying. She sighed. "I don't want to tell you."

He raised an eyebrow but didn't insist. "As long as you'll still go with me to the concert." A hint of worry hung in his voice, flooding her heart with warmth.

"I do. I wouldn't want to miss seeing Andy Williams live on stage for anything in the world."

"You're tolerating me, because of him?" His mock indignation made her laugh, and she'd already thought of a saucy rebuke when she noticed a little black spot behind his ear. She leaned in to have a closer look and almost doubled over.

"... You have been telling the truth!"

"About what?"

Zara laughed heartily and rushed into the kitchen to grab a towel. When she returned with the wet towel in her hand, he held up his hands in mock defense saying, "I've done nothing."

"Haven't you told me yourself that you got into a fight and rolled in motor oil like a pig in mud? I'm just going to remove the evidence." With resolute steps she closed the distance between them and scrubbed the black spot from his skin.

He winced. "Hey, that hurts. Can't you be more caring and gentle?"

That man would be the death of her with his silly antics. She was sure he endured worse treatment every day in his job. Trying to keep a serious face, she said, "If you don't stand still, I'll wipe the spot away with my handkerchief, after spitting on it."

His eyes became wide and horrified. "You wouldn't do that, would you? No, don't say it, of course you would."

She grinned sardonically.

"My mother used to do this all the time when I was young. It was so icky." He made a grimace to emphasize his words.

"Women's spittle has a secret ingredient that cleans the dirt simple water and soap cannot." She giggled.

He caught her hand that was holding the towel and locked eyes with her. "Instead of using your miracle spittle on a towel that is urgently needed to serve as candy parachute, you could remove any other spots you may find on my skin directly with your tongue. I wouldn't mind." He cocked his head to give her better access to his neck, while his face took on a dreamy expression.

"I'm sure you would like that." She had to suppress her giggles. "But in your case I'd rather resort to bleach and a scrubbing brush."

"You'll be the death of me, cruel lady. I really have no idea why I even go out with you." He gave a theatrical sigh.

"Because you're a scoundrel and love the challenge. And now let's go or we'll be late for Andy."

AFTER A FANTASTIC SHOW, she allowed Glenn to take her out for a drink and when he returned her to the Gardners' house she didn't care whether anyone could see them or not as she let him kiss her on the porch.

As soon as his soft yet rough lips touched hers, she completely forgot her resolve not to get involved and opened her lips. At first it was a slight shock when his tongue slipped inside to explore her mouth but just seconds later she relished the tingle running all the way down to her toes. Her entire body heated up and she pressed herself harder against him until someone harrumphed.

Her employers had returned home and stood a few feet away, wanting to unlock the front door. Zara felt herself flush beet red and was thankful for the darkness only lit by a solitary streetlamp, hiding her embarrassment.

"I'm...sorry," she mumbled and slipped inside without saying goodbye to Glenn. Then she rushed upstairs into her room and buried her head under the pillow. Kissing as if there was no tomorrow on her employer's front porch!

26

ZARA

Zara had been avoiding Cath for as long as she could, but working for her and living in the same house made this a very awkward situation. After speaking to her only when absolutely necessary for two days, Cath finally took her aside. "We need to talk."

"I'm sorry, it won't happen again," Zara apologized.

"Let's sit down." Cath accompanied her to the library where they both settled into the armchairs. "It's none of my concern whether you have a boyfriend or not."

Zara breathed again. "You're not going to fire me?"

"Not unless you neglect your duties." Cath smiled. "I have grown to like you and I would hate to see you get hurt. But despite his often reckless attitude, Glenn's a good man."

"I never wanted to start a relationship with Glenn, but he's pretty persistent."

"He can be when he wants to. Charles and Glenn have been friends for many years, but so far, he's never been like this with a woman. I think he's serious with you."

"Oh no! I'm definitely not interested in anything serious," Zara protested. When she noticed how awful those words sounded, especially after being caught making out with a friend of the family on their front porch, she added, "I mean, I really like him. He's a nice guy, and we have lots of fun together but I'm just not ready to get married."

"Nobody is talking about marriage." Cath laughed. "We're not living in the nineteenth century anymore. Believe it or not, nowadays women are allowed to have a boyfriend and even to kiss passionately without having to marry. Although I would prefer if you didn't do it in front of my house."

Zara's cheeks heated up with shame. Her father would have taken his belt to her if he'd seen her like that, and her mother... would probably have died of disgrace. "It won't happen again. I promise."

"On the other hand, it's nice to see you happy. You never told me what exactly happened during your time under Soviet arrest, nevertheless I could feel your pain." Cath put a hand on Zara's arm. "All of us need to care for someone and be cared for. This doesn't have to be a lover, it can be anyone, family, friends, patients, students, or children. Since you came here devoid of family or friends, I have seen how you started to care for my children, and how they have grown to love you."

Zara nodded.

"But now, maybe it is time to let yourself be weak and have someone care for you. Someone to ask about your day, make you laugh when you're sad, brighten your day with a little surprise, and give you something to look forward to. True love isn't about heated kisses and fierce passion, although this is a nice part of it." Cath gave a dreamy smile. "True love is knowing there's someone who will stand by your side and support you always. Together, life is so much easier and more enjoyable than going it alone. And there's no rush in it. Charles and I went steady for almost a year before we even kissed, although that was a long time ago, when we both were still kids. And look at us now, despite having two children and having been separated by the war for years, we're still as much in love as we were on the first day. We may fight once in a while, but that doesn't change anything, it only adds to the strength of our relationship. I want you to allow yourself the chance of being loved, too."

"Thank you." Zara had a lot to think about, and the more she thought about Cath's words, the more she realized that she had fallen in love with Glenn. Not that she would tell him.

Her heart beat faster at the realization and for the first time in years she felt free, without a single care in the world. Cath was right, with Glenn by her side, nothing was insurmountable.

27

GLENN

"Goodbye, sweetheart," Glenn said, and gave Zara a passionate kiss before he helped her out of the car on this gray November evening.

"I'll miss you," she said and pressed herself against him. Since that concert so many things between them had changed. Zara still balked at the idea of making their relationship official, but he didn't care. As long as she agreed to go out with him, he would be the happiest guy on earth.

"It's just for three days until my schedule rotates again. I'll pick you up on Thursday at six p.m."

"Three days are much too long," said the girl who pretended she didn't want to commit, with a pout. "Take care and fly carefully."

It was a strange thing, but it actually felt good to have someone fussing over him. "I always do."

She laughed. "I know for a fact that you don't. Aren't you the man whom they call reckless and who is known for his shenanigans in the air?"

"Pahhh... that's just jealousy. The other pilots would love to have my skills in the air."

"At least you don't suffer from low self-esteem. I really have to go now." She pressed another hot kiss on his lips. It was an entirely unfamiliar feeling for him but he could barely break loose from her. Three days was a very long time indeed.

He drove back to the airbase to start his first of three night-shifts and half an hour later he jumped into the cockpit with a huge smile on his face. The weather was perfect, a cold but cloudless night, and he itched to fly under the star-spattered sky. He loved the night flights, when the aircraft traveled across silent lands bathed in starlight. After dozens of return tours he knew the route by heart, had memorized every single beacon and even the landing approach by heart.

At times he thought his hands could do the job, even while he was asleep. It would be an easy flight. Pure joy. Since no turbulence was predicted, he could dream about Zara on the way. One day he'd take her with him and show her just how beautiful it was above the clouds.

His co-pilot, Teddy, and his trusted flight engineer, Gus, as well as the navigator, Rick, were in a similar good mood throughout the takeoff procedures. They were scheduled for three back-to-back flights until the day crew took over in the morning.

Once at cruising altitude, Glenn relaxed in his seat, thinking of Zara and how much he had grown to like her. It had been a very unexpected experience. In the beginning, he'd pursued the thrill of the chase, but it had evolved into so much more, and now his first thought in the morning was about her, as was his last one before falling asleep.

She was definitely different than all the other girls he'd gone out with. He hesitated to call it love; love was such a big word, but he cared about her very much, more than was good for either of them, because in the not-so-distant future he'd be rotated back stateside or someplace else. What would happen to her then? *To us*, he corrected himself.

There were only two possible endings to this. First, he could simply forget about her, although his heart squeezed at the thought of never seeing her again. Second, he could marry her and take her with him. This time it was his stomach that squeezed at the thought of being trapped in marriage.

Unfortunately, there was no in-between.

"What's up?" Teddy asked.

"Nothing." Glenn returned his mind to the present and to the beautiful sight of the landscape beneath him, sparkling rivers and lakes that reflected the moonlight, dark forests on rolling hills as they approached the Fulda beacon, the last mark before entering the Soviet zone.

"Problems with your girl?"

"Nah...we're good."

"So...thinking about what will happen when you're rotated?"

"You're a shrink now? I'm perfectly fine, so stop butting into my private life." Teddy was a great pal, and the best co-pilot ever, but even with him Glenn wouldn't discuss his confusing emotions toward Zara. Teddy had a wife and two children back home and wouldn't understand.

Moments later they flew into the southern corridor, and Glenn grabbed the yoke tighter. There weren't any strong winds forecasted, but all the same it wouldn't help to deviate from the course and anger the Russians.

"Oh shit," muttered Teddy.

Even before he finished speaking, Glenn was dazzled by a powerful searchlight. "Stupid hoodlums in action again!" he groused, squinting his eyes. While he could fly the route blind, just by memory and with the help of his instruments, it was an annoyance having to deal with this shit.

"Soviets playing war again," Teddy commented, when beneath them anti-aircraft guns erupted. Despite the knowledge that their altitude was much too high for the bullets to cause damage, it was unnerving to say the least.

"If these crooks believe we'll be scared into returning home, they're on the wrong track," Glenn said, wondering what the Russians were trying to achieve with their stupid antics. No pilot in his right mind flying in a string of thirty to forty other aircraft in ninety-second intervals would be stupid enough to turn around inside the small corridor. Or did they actually think the Americans would disrupt their air traffic just because of a few ack-acks?

He grabbed the yoke tighter and kept the Skymaster on course, while he warned air control both in Berlin and Wiesbaden about the Soviet activity.

"And here I thought this would be a nice and quiet flight in the moonlight," he joked after telling his crew to be on alert.

"Yak coming in from three o'clock," Teddy shouted.

Damn! Glenn would gladly engage in a dogfight with the Soviet fighter craft any time of the day, but not at the yoke of a clunky, slow and heavy cargo plane without weapons on board. He wished for the trusted Tomahawk fighter he'd flown during the war to give the damn Yak a piece of his mind.

Despite knowing the bloody Yak wouldn't actually shoot at them, it was still unnerving. The Yak approached close enough to see the face of its pilot, who smirked at them, before he finally changed course and went about twenty feet above Glenn, who hadn't deviated a single inch from his course.

"I hope we've seen the last of him," Teddy said.

Glenn wiped the sweat from his forehead with the back of his hand. "I'm not so sure. They'll probably use the clear weather conditions to annoy the hell out of us."

And he was right, because only thirty seconds later the Russian had turned his Yak around and came at them again.

"He's back," warned Teddy.

"Yep. Saw him." Glenn wished he could simply turn his

Skymaster into the Yak's path, waiting for the fighter pilot to chicken out. But he knew that General Tunner would chew his ass for being reckless and endangering not only the lives of his own crew, but also those of the following aircraft in the block.

Since the official policy was not to anger the Soviets, he kept his cool and barreled on, keeping his machine straight on course to Tempelhof Airport.

"What a foolish move, he's coming directly at us," Teddy yelled with alarm in his voice.

"Shit!" Glenn screamed as the Yak didn't turn away, and he frantically jerked the yoke to swing his aircraft around, but the fully loaded Skymaster was much too heavy to react quickly and Glenn watched in slow motion as the Yak crashed frontally into his left wing.

"Mayday! Mayday!" he shouted into the intercom. "Buzzing Yak crashed into us. Going down!" He gave his last position, before he had his hands full, trying to control the heavy aircraft corkscrewing downwards in ever faster circles until it plunged into the ground.

28

VLADI

Vladi was lying in bed nursing an awful hangover when someone knocked on the door of his quarters in the Karlshorst barracks. He glanced at the alarm clock on his nightstand. Ten a.m. May the person who dared to wake him at this ungodly hour rot in eternal purgatory.

"Come in," he growled, heaving himself up from the bed.

It was Colonel Ulyanin's personal aide. Since it wouldn't do Vladi any favors to be disgruntled about being woken up or ask the aide about the reason for this unexpected visit, he curbed his anger and managed to say in a civil tone, "How can I help you?"

"The colonel is expecting you in his office."

Vladi groaned inwardly. He'd had the intention of making himself scarce at the SMAD headquarters until General Sokolov came down from his rampaging foul mood. "I'll be right there."

"I was instructed to drive you in the car."

The day slowly progressed into a veritable hell. Would that overzealous puppet make sure Vladi got properly dressed and shaved? "I'll be downstairs in five minutes."

Much to his relief, the aide nodded. "Five minutes at most. The colonel said it was very urgent."

What kind of shit could be so important to justify rousing him from slumber in the early morning and ordering him into the office of some colonel who wasn't even his boss? Ulyanin might command the Soviet Air Force in Berlin, but he had no say over members of Red Army Intelligence.

He should simply refuse to cooperate with Ulyanin and go back to sleep. If this idiot needed help, he should go through official channels.

As if reading his mind, the aide turned in the doorway and said, "Comrade Propov has approved of your assistance in this matter."

Vladi's mood plummeted further. His son-of-a-bitch boss hadn't seen the necessity of informing him. If it was true that the sycophant had agreed to whatever this matter was, there wasn't much Vladi could do, except to show his defiance in another way.

He stared at his freshly ironed uniform hanging at the door and smirked as he turned toward his locker and instead slipped into his personal uniform of black pants, black shirt and the worn leather jacket.

Rubbing a hand across his hair instead of brushing it, he forwent his morning shave and provocatively opened the top two buttons of his shirt to expose his abundant chest hair. He wouldn't normally attend an official meeting like this, since he used this look when on the prowl for a new girl, but he itched to show the spick-and-span, prissy colonel exactly what he thought about being summoned like this.

The aide waited inside the car, a remnant of the American lend and lease program, which was quite ironic and made Vladi smile for the first time this day. He flopped onto the passenger seat and barely hid a satisfied grin when he saw the young soldier's disapproving frown.

Of course, a career soldier who'd never been in combat – the most dangerous thing he'd ever done probably was to put a knife-sharp crease into his uniform trousers – valued a slick appearance over everything else.

Vladi lit himself a cigarette without offering one to the man behind the steering wheel. The bootlicker would need both hands on the wheel in the correct ten-two position anyway to satisfy his need for sanitized correctness.

Neither of them spoke a word and five minutes later, Vladi jumped out of the car in front of the SMAD without so much as a thank you. He hadn't got his reputation for being a rabble-rouser by being polite, and this prim and proper baby needed a reminder who Captain Rublev was.

In late autumn the premises looked absolutely stunning, if one was prone to that kind of kitsch. Vladi wasn't, although he'd learned to pretend, since it always pleased the ladies when he whispered sweet words about the beauty of the leaves on the trees glowing in every imaginable yellow, orange and red hue. He shrugged. Getting sentimental wasn't something he ever wanted to be.

He desperately needed a good old-fashioned brawl, beating up someone, or he'd soon turn into a slick, fastidiously sharp-looking career soldier with creases in his uniform trousers. To make up for the softness in his mood, he straightened his shoulders, snapped a salute at the sentry and walked up the stairs to the second floor with a grim expression on his face.

Colonel Ulyanin met him halfway up the staircase. "Comrade Captain, good to see you."

Vladi frowned. "It's my pleasure, Comrade Colonel."

"Let's go. I'll brief you in the car."

What the heck? Vladi felt the vein in his temple pulsating violently at the disrespectful treatment. He wasn't some foot soldier who had to dance to the colonel's tune. He was about to give a terse answer when the colonel preempted him and said, "This is an official request, coming directly from Sokolov."

"I'm all ears, Comrade."

Once settled in the backseat of the car that had been waiting with its engine running, Ulyanin let the cat out of the bag. "We have an American pilot in our custody."

"Here in Berlin?" That was an outrageous breach of the Potsdam agreement, not that he cared about diplomatic agreements, but the official directive had been to annoy the heck out of Americans, while stopping short of violating any important agreement for fear of causing them to mobilize their army and march on Berlin.

Since the traffic restrictions had been put in place months ago, the Americans had prohibited their soldiers from entering the Soviet sector, therefore Vladi wondered how they'd gotten the man.

"Of course not. About eight hours ago, an American C-54 crash-landed in our territory. All crew members except for the pilot died. He was transported to our military hospital near Erfurt."

That was terrific news and had the potential to make up for the lost morning sleep. For a moment Vladi regretted not having put on his uniform, if he was to meet and possibly question an American pilot. "Is he conscious?"

"He wasn't when the hospital called my office, but the doctors were confident that he will be once we arrive there."

"We are going to Erfurt?"

"Yes."

"Your aide should have warned me. I haven't even had breakfast." He glowered at the back of the head of the young soldier in the driver's seat.

Ulyanin handed him a sandwich that looked like it had been in the car for at least a week. "This will have to do. We can stop to grab a bite once we arrive in Erfurt."

Vladi wanted to pummel his fists into the metal car door. Why did these missions always turn into nightmares? Why couldn't Sokolov find another man to do his dirty work? And dirty work it would be, he was sure about that.

Interrogating an American soldier –questioning, he corrected himself – constituted a severe blow against what was left of the Soviet-American friendship and could easily lead to a major diplomatic catastrophe, should the Americans get whiff of it. Naturally, all the fault would be piled up on Vladi's shoulders and send him to Siberia before he ever had his damned breakfast.

As much as he normally loved his role as rabble-rouser, today was not one of those days. Pondering the situation once more, he concluded it might come in handy that he hadn't put on his uniform. The American didn't have to know Vladi was Soviet military, he could pretend to be a rogue German working in the hospital. Vladi's German was certainly good enough to fool one of the American nitwits.

He'd devise an action plan later, because right now he had to tease out every last morsel of information from Ulyanin, and food. Working on an empty stomach wasn't his thing, so he decided to bite into the offered sandwich and immediately regretted doing it. It tasted as dry as sawdust. "What is this?"

"No idea. It's from a West Berlin bakery. We use them as examples of how much better people are off in our sector," Ulyanin said, his eyes twinkling with delight at Vladi's suffering.

Vladi was sure anyone forced to eat the sawdust sandwich would change sides with flying colors. "What do you want from me?"

Ulyanin gave him a sarcastic side-glance. "Comrade Propov was right, you're the perfect man for this mission. I was hesitant at first, but given your appearance…"

"I'm not used to being woken in the middle of the night and summoned to someone's office," Vladi quipped.

Ulyanin ignored his objection and continued, "Less than six hours after the accident, the vicious imperialists have officially requested permission to retrieve their crew. They have doctors and an ambulance waiting at the zonal border."

"I see."

"We had to inform them about the crash, which they already knew about, and we delayed confirming the discovery of the crew members as long as possible. But you know how those pesky capitalists are. Thinking we have nothing better to do than answer their inquiries."

Vladi nodded. Ulyanin would be on the red phone within the blink of an eye, should one of his aircraft crash in the American zone.

"How did that happen anyway?"

Ulyanin grimaced. "I lost one of my best fighter pilots, because of this incident."

"I see." The picture in Vladi's mind was clear: a Yak fighter had buzzed the American cargo plane and the young and reckless pilot had taken it too far. Military strategists were already working on the best way to blame the American machine for the incident.

"Anyhow, we told the Americans that the pilot, Captain Glenn Davidson, survived while the rest of the crew didn't. They were adamant in getting him back, but we told them he's still unconscious and not transportable. Our doctors will give them progress reports when something changes."

"How did they take it?" Knowing the Americans, Vladi couldn't imagine they would simply stand by and wait for Soviet doctors to dote on their patient. Even though everyone knew that Soviet medicine was by far the most advanced in the world and this airman could consider himself lucky to have crashed in their territory and not, let's say, over France.

"Not good. They were adamant about sending their doctors to be with him, even if he wasn't in a condition to be transported home."

"Understandable," Vladi said, and Ulyanin glowered at him.

"We couldn't flat-out deny their request so we covered them up in red tape. Told them we first have to get approval from military headquarters. And you know how slow they can be making decisions. I hear General Sokolov is not available right now," Ulyanin said with a malign grin. "That should give us at least three days to ask Davidson some questions. But I have to warn you, there must not be any injuries that couldn't have been a result of the crash."

Vladi understood all too well. The American doctors would scrutinize the patient and even if they didn't find anything suspicious he would tell them about his treatment, if he survived. Nobody wanted a major diplomatic incident, so Davidson had to be treated with kid gloves or perish in the process.

"What exactly do you want to find out from him?"

The colonel made an overemphatic hand movement. "Everything. How and where they do the maintenance on their aircraft, how they achieve such a low accident rate, etc. Anything that might expose a weakness. But mostly I want to know about the inner workings of the operation, and how they cope with bad weather. I need to know everything about that new radar system they're working on, ground controlled approach, and instrument flight. There must be a weak point somewhere that we can use to our advantage."

"Why don't you just wait for autumn to do its work and shroud Berlin in a layer of fog? Remember last year when that awful soup was so thick we couldn't see our own hands in front of our eyes?"

"The weather is not under my command, so I'd rather not rely on its cooperation."

There was nothing to add and Vladi sunk back into silence, pondering how to question a badly injured, probably unwilling person whom he had to treat with utmost caution. It wouldn't be easy and he had to rely on luck, or... "Can the doctors give him something to make him talk?"

"That was my first thought, too, but the doctors said no. For whatever medical gibberish, it's not an option in this case."

Shit! If Davidson didn't cooperate there was only one solution left. "What if he succumbs to his injuries before the American doctors arrive? Would that work?"

"I'd rather not have him die on my watch, but if it's absolutely necessary, then you do what you must. Just make sure nobody finds out."

The car steered off the Autobahn and minutes later parked in front of a beautiful Renaissance villa that had been converted into a military hospital. Vladi was always surprised to find such a gem in an otherwise heavily destroyed German city. Since the Moscow administration funneled everything of worth, including construction material, into the Soviet Union as reparations, there never was material on hand to repair the damages sustained during the war.

Unfortunately, East Germany had to bear the brunt of the reparations, because the other Allies had put a foot down and stopped the reparations coming from their zones. It was a very selfish way to pay back the huge sacrifices Russians had made to win the Great Patriotic War with very little help from the other Allies, who'd been hiding out in England, waiting until it was safe for them to cross the Channel.

The capitalist thugs wouldn't even allow a quadripartite ruling over the Ruhrgebiet with its precious resources of black coal that were of much higher quality than the brown coal found in the Soviet occupied zone. Vladi grumbled. *Thieves and crooks!* Pretending to be benefactors to Germany, when all they wanted was to keep the black coal for themselves.

They had illegally stopped the agreed deliveries of coal to Russia, just because some hoodlums in Poland — over whom Moscow had no jurisdiction whatsoever — had stolen a few of the freight cars. Vladi empathized with the Poles, who'd suffered harshly under the Nazi oppression, before the Soviet Union had come to liberate them.

"Time for breakfast," Ulyanin announced.

Vladi glanced at his wristwatch – liberated from its German owner years ago. It was past three p.m. and his stomach was rumbling viciously. He just hoped the hospital canteen would have better food than the sawdust sandwich Ulyanin had given him earlier. If he didn't get acceptable food into his stomach soon, the American would have to suffer for it.

29

ZARA

Heavy shopping baskets in both hands, Zara walked back from the grocery store to the Gardners' home. It was only a five-minute walk, but with the bags it seemed to stretch endlessly and she had to pause every now and then to put the bags on the ground before continuing her trip.

Before the currency reform, it had been next to impossible to buy anything with Reichsmark and people had used US dollars or cigarettes instead. She'd always imagined that the Allied soldiers and their families swam in luxuries, because they had an apparently never-ending supply of hard foreign currency.

But Cath had told her that even with dollars it had often been impossible to buy what she needed and they'd had to go to the PX store to buy supplies shipped in from the United States.

This had changed almost overnight with the currency reform, when like a miracle *Bückware*, the under-the-counter-goods, appeared on the shelves available for anyone who was in possession of the new Deutsche Mark.

Zara would have loved to witness this historic point in time but she had been in Hohenschönhausen...the panic following this thought attacked her out of the blue. A heavy weight pressed down on her, making it difficult to breathe. Her vision swam and little black stars danced in front of her eyes. She gasped for breath, setting down the heavy bags, before she crouched on the ground like a fetus, focusing on a dandelion growing at the curb.

After a while, the weight on her chest eased up and she could breathe again. These panic attacks were frightening, but with time she had learned to live through them. One day, she hoped, they would simply go away.

Staggering upright, she took hold of a garden fence, before bending down again to grab the shopping bags. That's when she heard a familiar voice say, "Are you all right, Zara?"

Her blood froze and she couldn't move, stuck halfway between crouching and standing, unable to even lift her head and look at the person she hadn't seen in such a long time.

As she focused on a red tomato in her grocery basket, the shock subsided and rage boiled up in her. The audacity to come here! To show up in plain sight, to compromise her, to make her a target of whoever was after him. It was another example of his self-centeredness and absolute lack of care for anyone beyond himself.

The rage took possession of her, flooding any remnant of stiffness from her limbs. She left the bags where they were and straightened her back, doing a half-turn to face the man. The observation that with her modest heels she towered over him gave her courage and strength.

"What do you want?"

He was taken aback, definitely not pleased, and his right eyelid twitched angrily. "Is this any way to greet your father?"

Not long ago she would have cowered in fear of him, but that time was gone for good. She might have to thank her

Soviet interrogators for freeing her of the bonds her father had
held her in during all her life.

"I don't want anything to do with you. You left me and
Mother to fend for ourselves and cravenly escaped the country." She glared at him, the bottled-up emotions of years
coming to the surface. Pictures zipped through her mind in fast
motion. From his condescending ways when she was a child
and he'd always told her she was "just" a girl, not to be
compared with her much worthier brothers, to the times he'd
proudly boasted about her achievements at the *Bund Deutscher
Mädel*, as if it were somehow his doing, to the one time when
she'd visited him at the concentration camp and he'd harshly
told her it was wrong to feel sympathy for these creatures
because they were criminals who deserved their treatment, to
the last time she'd seen him.

That was a Wednesday in late April 1945 when she'd caught
him packing his suitcase and had asked, "Are we leaving before
the Russians come?"

"The Russians will never get here and you are safe."

"And you, why are you leaving?" She had pointed at his
suitcase.

"I'm going on a business trip and will be back for the
weekend at the latest."

"Why can't I come with you?" Like every woman in
Germany, she'd heard about the behavior of the Russian
soldiers and was afraid.

"Because business is for men. You do what I say." Then he'd
turned around and left the house. She hadn't seen him since,
not until today, more than three years later.

Back then, she had believed him. And he'd been right, a
week later it wasn't the Russians who arrived, but the Americans. Zara's mother committed suicide and Zara had been
forced by the new masters to bury thousands of emaciated
corpses in the Mauthausen camp.

She shrugged off the images attacking her. What she had seen was...she still couldn't believe it had been her father's doing, and she could believe even less that he'd never shown a hint of empathy or guilt. In hindsight that moment had been the pivotal point in her life, when she'd stopped believing the Nazi propaganda and her father's words.

"You must understand, I had to leave. It was too dangerous for me to stay," her father pleaded with her.

"You're a coward, unwilling to bear the consequences of your disgraceful actions!"

"How dare you!" he spat out, taking a step toward her. But if he expected her to back down, he was very much mistaken.

"Why are you here?" she asked him with ice in her voice, the hot rage seeping from her body, leaving only indifference behind about her last remaining family member.

"Because I wanted to see my only daughter," he said with a slick smile. Always the handsome man, charming his counterparts into doing whatever he wanted. It had worked with everyone for as long as she could remember. But it wouldn't work now.

"It took you three and a half years to find out that you're yearning to see me again?" She laced her voice with sarcasm, stretching her spine a bit more to look down on him.

He gave a start. She had never contradicted him before, and even now she felt bad about doing it. He was her father after all, and children had to obey their parents.

"I wanted to, but it wasn't safe." He shrugged, looking contrite.

"For you or for me?"

"Why are you so angry? I came here because I love you."

She'd struggled for his love twenty long years. Her entire life had been an attempt to please him, to gain his appreciation. Now that he'd finally said the words, they didn't mean anything to her. "Did you know that the Soviets arrested and tortured me to find out your whereabouts?"

"It wasn't my fault." He didn't even flinch.

"Of course it was! If you had given up yourself, they wouldn't have been after me!" she yelled at him.

"*Schatzi...*"

"Don't *Schatzi* me! I paid for your crimes because you were too much of a coward to take responsibility."

"This is no way to talk to your father!" The vein pulsating in his neck was a sure sign of his fury. As a child she'd feared his temper. He'd ruled his family with an iron fist. Usually her brothers had been at the receiving end of his palm or belt, but she'd experienced them several times, too.

Out of habit she ducked her head, ready to appease him, when the rage inside her bubbled up again like the gas in a shaken Fanta bottle. She took a step backwards and glanced around. A mother with three small children walked toward her and a couple of American soldiers were sitting at the bakery where she and Glenn often visited to drink coffee and eat one of those delightful sweets.

Thoughts of Glenn made her heart warm and gave her the courage to confront her father. She would not back down from her father ever again. Nothing he might do to her could compare to what she'd already endured at the hands of the Russians. "When you left me to fend for myself at the end of the war, you forfeited your privilege to call yourself my father."

It felt incredibly empowering to say these words. Severing her ties to him didn't make her feel in the least sad or distressed. On the contrary, it was as if someone had taken a millstone from around her neck and she felt light as a feather, ready to float away in a bubble of bliss.

She was free at last!

"You don't really mean this," he said.

"Look, the Soviets are still after you and so are probably the Americans. If I were you I'd go to wherever you have been for the past three years and never return to Germany again. Or, if you want to do the right thing for once in your life, you could turn yourself in," she said, impassively, devoid of any emotion she might still have had for him five minutes ago, since all she wanted was to have him gone — for good. She didn't care what he did or didn't do, as long as he never showed up in her life again.

"Actually, I wanted to propose a deal to the Americans and since you're working for Colonel Gardner, I thought you could help me."

"And here I thought you came because of your undying love and yearning for your only daughter, but no, you want me as go-between to the American Military administration?" For some reason, she suddenly felt dirty.

"I have information they want, but I need to get a deal in writing with them before I show up. I can't risk their arresting me and forcing me to spill the beans without getting anything back in return."

"What could possibly be so important for them to guarantee your safety instead of sending you to the Nuremberg trials where all your criminal friends have been tried and hanged?"

"Art. Incredibly valuable art. Something the world has been searching for for years," he bragged.

"Art you stole from the Jews, I assume. I don't want to…"

"You're stupid. You could be a hero. This is huge…" he called after her, but she'd already grabbed the grocery bags and was walking with her head high down the street. "If you want to find me, ask the baker for Josef Heindel," he called after her.

30

GLENN

White fog. Glenn blinked, but the white fog didn't vanish. Something was wrong and he struggled, trying to get up but he couldn't move his legs. He wasn't even sure they were still there. Blinking again, dark shadows appeared in his vision. He felt worse than with a full-blown hangover, almost as if he'd been run over by a train...or crashed with his aircraft.

Memory returned. The Yak coming straight at them, the crash, the tumbling aircraft. Then nothing. He blinked again. Slowly his vision was returning, but he still couldn't move. *Where am I*?

That question was answered when the door opened and a beautiful young nurse entered the room. At least he believed her to be a nurse because she was wearing a white uniform.

"You are awake, Captain Davidson. How are you feeling?" Her English was good, but with an odd accent he couldn't quite place.

"How do you know my name?"

In response she giggled. "How are you feeling?"

"Where am I?"

"In a hospital." She approached him to take his pulse.

"Which hospital?"

"Our hospital."

"I need to report to the American military base at Wiesbaden." He was getting exasperated, wanting to get up again, but his body refused to obey.

She put a hand on his shoulder and softly pressed him into the pillows, before giving him a stern glance and saying, "No more talking. You need rest."

Then she vanished from the room like a ghost and once the door had closed behind her noiselessly he wondered whether she had only been a product of his imagination.

Perhaps he was unconscious and dreaming? Pinching his arm would help to decide, but he couldn't move his arms either. They seemed to be restrained. *Am I in prison? And why?*

The nurse's perfume lingered in the air, making his nose tingle. Sniffing closely, it smelled more like disinfectant than perfume. In any case, Glenn took it as a sign that he wasn't dreaming because never before had he dreamed up smells. He must have fallen asleep again, because when he opened his eyes once more there was a man standing in his room.

"You're awake," he said in halting English with a very distinct Russian accent. "How do you feel?"

Why do they all say the same things? Annoyance crept into Glenn, and despite the negativity of the emotion he took it as a good sign to feel something again. "I want to talk to the American Military Administration."

The man in white — a Russian military doctor, Glenn presumed — smiled kindly. "General Clay has been informed about the unfortunate accident of your plane."

An accident your people caused. "Where are my crew?"

"I don't know." It was an obvious lie, but Glenn had dealt with enough bloody Russians to know the man wouldn't tell him anything.

"When can I go home?"

"You're not in any shape to be transported just yet, but don't worry, you're in the best hands with us, while we are awaiting further instructions."

No doubt you're not in a hurry to repatriate me. Glenn sighed. His entire body was hurting and he wasn't in a shape to get into an argument with this doctor. His best option was to play along and wait. His superiors knew his aircraft had crashed and supposedly they also knew that he and hopefully the rest of the crew were alive.

"What are my injuries?"

The doctor seemed much more comfortable talking about strictly medical topics and even warmed up, showering Glenn with a gush of words explaining every imaginable injury under the sun, ranging from broken ribs, flesh cuts, burns, to a concussion. Then he proceeded to do all kinds of experiments testing Glenn's reflexes until at last he held up a pencil in front of Glenn's eyes, while Glenn had to close first one eye and then the other.

"Your brain is fine. The rest will heal. With time." Someone knocked on the door and the doctor hurried to open it. He disappeared for a few minutes and when he returned, his face showed disapproval.

"The military police are here, they want to ask you a few questions to reconstruct how the accident occurred."

Glenn nodded, even though he didn't have the slightest intention of telling them anything except that their stupid Yak had caused the crash. The doctor looked as if he wanted to say something but then simply shrugged and left the room, leaving the door open for two military policemen and one woman in civilian clothes to enter.

"Captain Davidson?"

"Yes."

"We are here to ask you a few questions."

"I heard."

"Can you please give us a detailed description of what happened directly before your plane crashed?"

"Where is my crew?"

An uncomfortable silence ensued and Glenn got the impression there was something they didn't want to tell him, so he asked once more. They conversed in Russian and finally the woman said, "Unfortunately you were the only survivor."

The words punched him in the gut and he howled, "Murderers!"

The translator paled, but caught herself right away and blanked her expression. "It was an accident and our people rescued you."

"An accident that was caused by your Yak buzzing my aircraft!" As soon as he finished his accusation, Glenn sank deeper into the pillows, completely out of breath from the effort.

"We don't know of any Yaks. We're here to investigate the circumstances of this accident," the military policeman had the audacity to say.

Glenn groaned. They could investigate whatever they wanted. If they didn't know about Yaks, he'd pretend not to know about aircraft in general.

"You were flying in the disputed air corridor over our territory."

Glenn would have jumped out of the bed, if his broken ribs hadn't kept him in place. "I don't remember."

"You don't remember what?" the translator asked with a slight tremble in her voice. Glenn didn't answer. "Do you remember flying over our territory?"

"I was on a flight to Berlin", he said without mentioning Tempelhof, but they would know this anyway.

"Why did you lose control over your aircraft?"

"I don't remember."

On and on the questions went, until the two military police looked at each other and one of them gave a barely perceptible shake of his head.

"We will ask you again, when you're in a better condition. Your brain needs rest for the memories to return," the translator said and the three of them left the room, much to Glenn's relief.

He had to get a clear head, before deciding what to do and how much to cooperate with the Soviets. Technically they were still allies, even though the Berlin blockade had heated up the divergent opinions to a point where war was in the air. Therefore, he considered himself to be in enemy territory and until he could talk to one of his superiors, he would behave accordingly.

Exhausted from the questioning he slipped back into sleep. When he woke up for the third time, a man in civilian clothes, wearing a black leather jacket over a black shirt, was sitting on a chair in the corner of his room and staring at him. The man looked slightly familiar, but Glenn couldn't quite place him.

"You're awake. How do you feel?" the stranger asked in passable English as he stood up.

"How ingenious!"

"I'm sorry?"

Glenn rolled his eyes. "What do you want?"

The man gave a nervous nod toward the door and said, "Nothing. I just wanted to make sure you're okay."

"I'm sure about that."

"My nephew is crazy about planes. One of his favorite pastimes is plane-spotting, you know?" The man grinned. "He knows all the planes in existence, I believe."

Glenn didn't know what to make of this stranger. He didn't wear a uniform, but it seemed impossible that a random civilian could march into a military hospital — and Glenn assumed he was in a military hospital — and talk to the patients.

"You live here?" Glenn asked.

"Oh no, just visiting." The stranger sat down on the edge of the bed, and Glenn felt how his neck hair stood on end, warning him that something was amiss. "It's a rare occasion to see an American around here." Another nervous glance toward the door. "I shouldn't be here."

"You probably shouldn't."

"Maybe you can tell me something about your aircraft for my nephew? I know it was a C-54, but what kind of instruments do you have? Or do you fly by sight?"

The alarm bells rang. Glenn might have a concussion, but he wasn't stupid. "Who are you really? And why are you here?"

The man put up his palms. "It was worth a try. You can call me Vladi. I work for Red Army Intelligence and my task is to find out everything possible about your flight and the circumstances of your accident."

"They sent Intelligence for that reason?"

"Yep. Because you weren't very cooperative so far."

"I don't remember what happened, just that I crashed and then I woke up here."

Vladi stared at him for a long time, before he said, "I don't believe you. But that's a moot point. You'll give me all the information I want to know."

"What could that possibly be?" Glenn asked.

"I'm sure you can guess." Vladi stood up and strolled toward the door. "I'll let you rest and come back after you've had some food. Then the two of us will have a conversation, and I don't have to tell you what happens if I'm not satisfied with your answers."

"I'm a member of the US Air Force," Glenn protested.

"All the more reason to cooperate with me."

The shock sank deep as Glenn realized the Russians

wouldn't play nice. He was deep inside their territory, probably one hundred miles past the inner German border. There was no way anyone could come to his rescue, if the Soviets decided to play hardball. But he'd give them a good fight before spilling any valuable information.

Confronted with his possible demise soon, he thought of Zara. Her beautiful face and her wonderful smile brought back some of his lost courage. Until a frightening thought entered his mind. She would be livid if he missed their date. He cursed himself for not asking about the day. He hadn't the slightest idea how much time had passed since the accident. Next, he chuckled about his own stupidity. He had bigger problems than his girlfriend being peeved about a missed date.

31

ZARA

Humming a tune, Zara dusted the library. She hurried to finish, because Glenn would be coming in less than an hour to pick her up and she still had to change, put on some make up, brush her hair... She smiled at her own excitement. The three days without him had seemed like an eternity. Despite her resolve not to fall for him, she now realized she was madly in love.

Just as she was putting the nick-nacks back onto the shelves, she heard the door and curiously peeked into the hallway.

"Mr. Gardner, you're early today. Do you want me to prepare a quick dinner for you?"

He seemed tired and waved a hand. "No, thanks. Can we go to my study for a moment, please?"

Goosebumps arose on her arms at the sight of his severe expression. This was bad, really bad. She could feel it in her gut. He had never called her into his study before.

"Please sit," he said kindly, and her goosebumps intensified.

"You're going to fire me," she blurted out.

He looked befuddled and scratched his chin. "No, why would you say that?"

She squinted her eyes at him, suddenly getting a very crazy feeling in her stomach. "Then, what is the bad news?"

"I should have waited for Cath to arrive. I'm not good at this," he murmured, avoiding her eyes.

Now she was sure it had something to do with her father and she relaxed. Mr. Gardner didn't know that she couldn't care less if the Amis had arrested him.

The silence drew out like a wad of chewing gum, and the pain on his face became increasingly intense while he searched for the right words.

"It's okay. Just tell me," she urged him, but he only shook his head, having to compose himself.

After taking a deep breath he shook his head once again and then fixed his eyes on her. The overwhelming sorrow in them hit her in the gut, even before he spoke. This was not about her father.

Running away seemed like a good solution, or at least covering her ears. Whatever his news was, she didn't want to hear it, she was sure of that.

"Glenn's aircraft crashed in Soviet territory."

Zara wanted to scream, but no sound left her mouth. She must have stood frozen for several seconds, her mouth agape, before she remembered her manners and closed it again.

"Is he...?" She couldn't bring herself to finish her sentence.

"No. We received news that Glenn was the only survivor of the crew, but he's badly injured. They have taken him to a Soviet military hospital near Erfurt." The heavy weight that had been threatening to squash her fell down and she half expected to hear the thud when it crashed onto the floor.

"He's alive." She stated the obvious, looking at Mr. Gardner for help.

"He is. But he's in critical condition and cannot be transported. He will have to remain in Soviet custody for the time being."

Zara nodded understanding, despite not grasping what he was saying. "Can I see him?"

Mr. Gardner snorted. "Our headquarter already requested permission to send one of our medical teams to help with treating Glenn and..." He broke off mid-sentence and Zara had the feeling there was something he didn't want to tell her. Something awful. Something the Russians might do if they weren't hindered by American officials.

"Are they going to harm him?" she said, absolutely aghast.

"No, of course not. He's a member of the US Air Force." He shook his head to emphasize his words. "Why would you even think that?"

Shivers ran down her spine at the memory of the events in Hohenschönhausen and now it was her turn to vigorously shake the head. "I don't know."

He came nearer and stared at her until understanding hit his face. "What did they do to you?"

She shrugged, not willing to talk about the sinister events. It was part of her past and would never happen again. That's why she had come to the American sector. To be safe from despotism and violence.

At that moment, Cath returned from a meeting with her army wives association and stumbled upon the peculiar scene: a visibly distressed husband and a sobbing housemaid in the study.

"What on earth has happened here?" she called out.

"Nothing," Mr. Gardner and Zara said in unison.

Cath furrowed her brows, looking pointedly from one to the other. "It looks like something to me."

"I'm sorry," Zara said, wiping the tears from her eyes.

"I just told her that Glenn's aircraft crashed in the Soviet occupied zone and he is in one of their hospitals, alive but in critical condition."

Cath put a hand to her mouth and her face became pale as a ghost. "When are you bringing him to Wiesbaden?"

"Headquarters is in the process of fighting the red tape to do so," her husband responded. "According to Soviet doctors he's not transportable."

"Oh. But I'm sure he'll come through just fine. The Soviets have good doctors," Cath said with a pitying glance toward Zara.

Much later, after dinner, Zara brought the children to bed and then returned downstairs to finish her chores. The Gardners were in a heated argument and when she heard her name, Zara stopped curiously on the stairs.

"Did you know that the Soviets tortured her during the interrogation?" Mr. Gardner asked.

"She never said so, always claimed they merely arrested her. Although, I did suspect that her story about falling down the stairs to explain her bruises was a lie, I thought of an abusive boyfriend she wanted to get away from. Never in my life would I have assumed the Soviet police did this."

"We need to let her go."

Thankfully Cath gasped in the same moment Zara did, so nobody heard her.

"Why?"

"She presents a danger, the Soviets are still looking for her," Mr. Gardner said.

"Are you telling me that you're afraid of the Russians? This is the American zone and we have the say here."

"Darling, it's a lot more complicated, and with the blockade and everything it's not a good idea to anger them."

"I never took you for a coward."

Zara hissed in a breath. What a bold statement to make to one's husband. Her own mother would never have dared to hurl such an insult at hers and neither would she have contradicted him on anything. Looking back, Zara realized that her mother had never voiced the slightest disagreement with her husband's decisions.

Mr. Gardner gave a deep sigh. "I'm just worried about you and the kids."

"I don't believe you. What is the real reason?"

A deep-throated harrumph cut through the air. "Look, my superiors have suggested using her as a way to get to her father should he try to contact her."

Zara threw a hand in front of her mouth at the same time as Cath shrieked, "And you miserable ruffian kept this a secret from me all this time?"

Despite the shocking revelation, Zara had to smile as she imagined how the woman pushed her lower lip forward and stood with arms akimbo, while insulting her husband with righteous indignation.

"I'm sorry, darling, I wasn't allowed to tell you."

"So why are you telling me now?"

"Because things are getting out of hand. All of this was planned before Zara got kidnapped, and then the blockade happened...she might still be under surveillance by the Soviets and..." He sighed. "If they connect her to Glenn, it won't help. They might assume he knows something, or they might use him as leverage to get information she is believed to have."

"She said her father never contacted her, and I believe her."

A hot flash ran through Zara's body. This had been true until two days ago. She swallowed hard. Did the Soviets know something? Would they torture Glenn to get her to hand over her father? She sank onto the stairs, burying her face in her hands.

"That woman presents a risk to my family. Do you even know what these Russians are capable of?"

"Are you afraid of the Soviets, Colonel Gardner?" The sarcasm was dripping from Cath's voice.

"Of course not."

"Then she stays. And that's my last word."

Zara had heard enough and used the opportunity to slip into the kitchen. The thoughts in her head were riding a carousel and she welcomed the distraction that cleaning the kitchen and washing the dishes provided. But later, in her bed, she couldn't sleep, since too much was going through her mind. Her sorrow about Glenn, but also the shocking truth that Mr. Gardner had employed her to find her father.

Again, she was nothing but a chess piece in the grander scheme of things. Where the Soviets hadn't succeeded with brutality, the Americans had used friendliness to get the desired result. She tossed around in her bed. Friendliness didn't hurt physically, but she still felt abused.

The fact that Cath hadn't known mollified her a bit, but then a horrible, momentous suspicion crept into her mind. Had Glenn been tasked with gaining her trust and weaseling information from her? Her heart seemed to explode as she entertained the thought. It couldn't be. Or could it?

Zara's head was hurting. Once the Amis repatriated him, she would coax Cath into getting her a permit to see him and then she'd confront him about her suspicion.

Since she couldn't sleep, she walked downstairs to heat some milk. Warm milk with honey always helped her to calm down and sleep. She was just about to pour the milk into the pot when a soft voice said, "You're still working?"

Startled, Zara all but dropped the pot. When she turned around she looked directly into Cath's face. "No. I couldn't sleep. Do you want some warm milk?"

"That would be nice."

Zara heated the milk and poured it into two mugs, putting a

teaspoon of honey into each one and stirring it thoroughly before handing one of the mugs to Cath. "Here you go."

"How are you holding up?" Cath asked as she took the mug and settled at the kitchen table.

"It's not like we had a serious relationship," Zara replied, despite the squeezing of her heart at the mere thought of Glenn lying alone and injured in a Soviet hospital.

Cath smiled knowingly. "I've never seen him as smitten with anyone as with you. He's a great guy once you get past the superficial mask he shows to the world."

Zara nodded. She'd grown fonder of Glenn the more she got to know him. "I'm sure he'll be fine."

"He will. He's a tough guy." Cath took a sip from her mug, pensive. "He loves you. Don't let anything get between you."

For lack of an answer, Zara nodded. Cath emptied her glass and said goodnight, but Zara stayed at the kitchen table for a long time staring at the wall until the solution hit her square in the face.

32

ZARA

She had been turning and tossing in her bed all night, trying to convince herself it was the right thing to do. It felt like betrayal, although she was merely helping justice along. He was her father, after all.

Nonetheless, he deserved to atone for his atrocious crimes against humanity. Deserved to be dragged before a military court and sentenced to whatever the judge deemed just.

In the morning she trudged downstairs and went through her chores like an automaton, looking horrible with the dark circles beneath her eyes. Cath gave her a single glance, before she said, "Take the day off. Go for a walk, eat a pastry, do anything to take your mind off him."

"Thank you," Zara said, grateful Cath didn't have the slightest inkling who actually had been on her mind most of the night, because it wasn't Glenn.

She walked upstairs to her room and rummaged with trembling hands in her drawer until she found the piece of paper with Vladi's phone number. She folded it twice and pushed it deep inside the pocket of her dress, where it immediately started burning a hole through the soft material.

The blue dress with a swinging skirt was a hand-me-down from Cath and since Zara was much taller than her employer, it showed a rather immodest amount of leg above her knee. Glenn had loved it when she was wearing this dress, and had always complimented her on her gorgeous legs. Warmth surged through her limbs at the memory of him wrapping her in his arms and swirling her around, before setting her down again and saying, "You look fabulous, sweetheart."

She shrugged the thoughts away. Now wasn't the time to get sentimental, since she had work to do. Putting on a coat, hat and gloves, she left the house and walked toward the town center, passing the first two public phone booths, before she found one that was standing around the corner of a huge building and was usually empty.

Her heart beating hard in her throat, she fidgeted with the piece of paper, barely able to unfold it. It was a number in Berlin and she wondered whether it would even work, since the phone connections between the American zone and East Berlin were sketchy at best.

Feeding the apparatus with ten *Pfennig*, she waited for the constant tone before she turned the dial plate. Twice, her finger trembled too much and she had to hang up the receiver and start all over again. After a while she heard the ringing in the line and the voice of a young man answered before the second ring. She almost hung up at the shock. This man definitely was not Vladimir Rublev.

"Hello, how can I help?"

"I want to talk to Captain Rublev, please."

"He's not here at the moment. Who is talking, please?"

She bit her lip, pondering what to tell him and finally said, "It's Zara. When will he be back?"

"I can't say."

Her heart sank. Vladimir was her best shot to get Glenn back. "Can you please tell him it's important? And urgent."

The man on the other side seemed to consider something and then said, "Can the captain call you back?"

She frantically searched for the number on the black apparatus, finally found it and gave it to him. "He can call me at this number. I'll be here this afternoon at three p.m."

The man made a tsking sound and she quickly added, "It's a public phone. I don't have a line in my house." It was a white lie, since the line in the Gardner's house didn't belong to her. But who cared about a little lie, when she was about to feed her father to the wolves?

She put down the receiver and stormed out of the telephone booth as if the devil incarnate were chasing her. *What have I done?*

At home, she met Cath, who had just returned from yet another meeting in her quest to collect donations for Little Vittles, and Zara jumped at the opportunity to ask her about Glenn.

Cath sadly shook her head. "I'm sorry but there's no news. The Soviets have agreed to deliver the deceased crewmembers to the border, but not Glenn. They are drowning us in red tape to get the permission to send our military doctors to look after him." She paused for a moment and after scrutinizing Zara's face, continued, "I probably shouldn't tell you this, but Charles is very worried about him. He fears the Soviets will use the opportunity to squeeze confidential information from Glenn."

Zara gasped and pressed a hand in front of her mouth. It was a lot worse than she had imagined, and merely thinking what Glenn might have to endure made her want to throw up. "Isn't there anything we can do to help him?"

"Short of barging into the Soviet zone with our army, we really can only wait for the diplomatic channels to do their work." She looked at Zara's miserable face and put an arm on her shoulder. "I know, you don't want to admit this, but it seems you're truly in love with Glenn."

Out of habit, Zara shook her head and put up her hands in protest, before she let them fall down again and said, "I guess you're right. Just thinking about how he must be suffering makes me suffer too."

"That is love. You would do anything for the other person. Love is a great thing and makes you incredibly happy, but it can also make you horribly sad."

Zara had never thought about it that way. How much must Cath have worried about her husband while he was away at war. "How did you cope?" she asked. "I mean all the years when Mr. Gardner was in Europe and you were back home with John?"

"It wasn't easy. It was... I felt every day like I was being put through the wringer. But I wouldn't want to miss one day of our marriage. Despite all the pain, the worry and the suffering, it was so worth it, every time we saw each other again."

Zara's heart melted. Her employer was putting into words what she'd been feeling all this time, but hadn't been able to voice. It felt as if her heart was bursting and all she could think about was Glenn. Although she couldn't very well tell Cath about her plans, she yearned for the approval of another loving woman for them. "I would do anything for him. Do you think that's wrong?"

"It's completely normal."

Although no details had been exchanged, Zara felt a lot more confident, because Cath had implicitly given her absolution to do whatever was needed to save Glenn.

Giddy with anticipation she waited with bated breath until Cath left to fetch her children. In that very moment, she rushed out of the house with a few coins in her pocket to dial Vladi's number in case he didn't call the public phone number she'd given him.

She arrived at the phone booth with two minutes to spare and was pretending to search for a number in one of the big yellow phone books hanging in a plastic holder, when a harsh ring cut through the silence inside the small cubicle.

The sound echoed off the glass walls and shocked her into rigidity. She stared at the black apparatus hanging from the wall, at the same time wishing it would ring again and that it would stop ringing. At the second ring she took up the receiver and held it against her ear. "This is Zara."

From the other end of the line she heard Vladimir's deep voice. "You wanted to talk to me." It was him, there was no mistaking the distinctive timbre of his voice.

"Yes. Is it safe to talk?" She didn't know what to expect, had never done this kind of secret work before.

"Safe for whom?" His voice betrayed his amusement. This man truly had a strange sense of humor.

"I wanted to suggest something but it is a delicate subject, if you understand."

"You finally agree to share my bed?" he chuckled into the phone and she felt herself blush from head to toe.

"I really need to talk to you in person." For some reason she felt as if a thousand pairs of eyes were upon her, even though the street was completely empty, except for a bunch of ragged children playing further down in the dirt.

"If it's not about you and me, then it must be about *him*."

She nodded, before she remembered that he couldn't see her and said, "Yes. It's complicated."

"I love complicated." For a good twenty seconds neither of them talked until she couldn't stay silent any longer.

"When can you be here?"

"You really do miss me, my darling."

She ignored his feeble attempts to charm her and said, "It will be worth your while."

"Well..." He paused again, but this time she endured the tension, desperately attempting not to seem too needy. "...I guess I could be in Wiesbaden by nine p.m."

"Tonight?" Zara stumbled against the wall of the phone booth, since she hadn't expected that kind of speed. "Aren't you in Berlin?"

"Nine p.m. At the park next to the train station. Find a bench by the fountain and wait for me." Then he hung up and she looked at the receiver in her hand with a million questions. The entire endeavor didn't seem like such a good idea anymore, but it was too late. Vladi was on his way to meet her.

In a dazed state she walked aimlessly around the town until it was time for dinner. Cath had warmed the remains of the potato casserole from the day before and grilled a T-bone steak for her husband and sausages for the children.

"I was worried about you," she greeted Zara.

"I was walking across town just like you suggested."

"Glenn will be fine. It's just a matter of time until the Russians will have to let him go." Glancing at Cath's concerned expression, Zara got the distinct feeling that nothing was fine and the Russians wouldn't let Glenn go, at least not alive.

"I'm sure everything will work out. Let me help you." Zara took the dishes from the cupboard and set the table.

Dinner would have been a somber affair, with the three adults worried about Glenn, if it weren't for John and Lisa, who kept talking non-stop about their day's adventures.

33

VLADI

After the phone call with Zara, he walked to the director of the military hospital and asked for a secure line to the SMAD.

"Comrade Propov, please," Vladi said into the phone.

"I'm sorry, but the Lieutenant Colonel is not here," the secretary answered.

Vladi put a hand across the receiver and uttered a string of curses. "How may I reach him? It's important."

"It will have to wait. He's on a retreat with Stalin – no disturbances."

Vladi groaned with despair. These top-secret retreats could last anything from a few hours to several days. "How long has he been there?"

"Not long. He left in the morning for Moscow."

"Thank you very much. Would you please let him know to give me a call at the Erfurt hospital as soon as it is convenient?"

"Certainly."

Vladi ran a hand through his hair. Things looked dire, since it was absolutely impossible to get ahold of his boss before he had to leave for Wiesbaden. The sensible course of action would be to stay and wait. In the Soviet Union individual initiative wasn't valued and one could never make a mistake by waiting for orders.

His orders were to interrogate Captain Davidson, which he had done – albeit without success. And he would do so again after he returned from Wiesbaden in the morning. Nobody would notice that he'd been absent for twelve hours or so. And if Zara indeed gave him information that would lead to her father's capture, he'd be a hero. He might even get a decoration, or at least the long overdue promotion. Weighing his options, he decided the risk of being found out was low in comparison to the possible benefits.

He already imagined himself as Major Rublev, bearer of the Order of the Red Star for the glorious capture of the abominable war criminal SS-Obersturmführer Ulbert.

Vladi's name would be on the headlines of all major newspapers across the Soviet Union and her brother nations. He would receive more money, more power, be invited to posh parties and, best of all, would be eligible for a private apartment in one of the neighborhoods in Moscow reserved for high functionaries when he finished his deployment to Berlin. Yes, it was a prize worth pursuing.

But he had to be secretive, since he couldn't risk that wastrel Captain Grusow getting wind of things and messing everything up, or worse, being successful and snatching the prize for himself.

Still doubtful about his decision, he snuck into Davidson's room. The pilot was fast asleep. The doctors had advised Vladi to wait with the interrogation until Davidson was stronger because that would yield better results. Looking at the sleeping man, Vladi knew it was now or never.

He slipped from the room, requested a car from the car pool and drove like a madman to the hotel room, where the office had sent his suitcase after it had become clear that he needed to stay a while in Erfurt.

Eying the selection of clothes, he discarded his uniform at once, and chose a smart gray business suit with brown shoes that would go perfectly with his false identity as a merchant living in Jena working for the Carl-Zeiss-Company.

He knew the Americans were keen to get their hands on the optical know-how of the German company and wouldn't prevent a merchant from crossing the border, even without proper papers.

Still, he opted to leave the Autobahn ahead of the zonal border and used a less-frequented crossing in one of the small villages. Just as he had banked on, the guard on the Soviet side bowed eagerly at the presentation of Vladi's military papers, while the guard on the American side winked him through after a mere glance at the nondescript car with Erfurt license plates and his hastily faked employee card for Carl-Zeiss.

If the guard had stopped him, he would have shown him his ID as a member of the Military Intelligence, who had the right to travel in all four zones, but that would have caused a whole slew of different problems – one of them being that they'd surveil his every step, and he really didn't have time for an elaborate action to lose his shadows.

During the drive he wondered what exactly Zara knew and what she wanted in return. He arrived in Wiesbaden just on time, parked the car, and rushed to the park to find her, slinging his coat tighter around him against the crisp and clear air. The cold season had arrived with full force, and while Wiesbaden had been spared, Berlin had been buried under a thick blanket of impenetrable fog.

The weather had indeed been kind to the Soviet people, the constant fog impeding the American and British efforts to land their planes in Berlin more often than not. Instead of the several thousand tons of a normal day, they had only been able to fly in a few hundred tons daily during the last two weeks.

Soon enough this unfortunate capitalist propaganda exploit would end, when the Western Allies had to accept that they couldn't provide for their own citizens in Berlin and would come begging for help from the Soviets. The great Soviet nation would step up to the task and shower the West Berliners with the wealth a vast network of brother countries could provide and everyone would be happy.

Once the capitalists realized that the people didn't buy in to their vile and amoral propaganda, the Western Allies would leave Berlin. With the capital freed from secessionists, German reunification was only a matter of time, and the warmongering Americans finally would pose no risk to the safety of the Soviet Union and all other peaceful communist countries anymore.

Uplifted by these reassuring thoughts, he whistled a tune as he approached the park, spotting Zara from far away, sitting on the bench near the fountain. Her long black hair faded into the darkness of the night, but she wore a beige woolen cap shining in the reflected light from the sky lit up by the nearby airbase.

"Hello, Zara," he said in German, startling her.

She clasped her handbag tight and looked around with that expression of a wounded fawn in her brown eyes. Once again, he was struck by how fragile she looked, when he knew she was anything but.

"Good evening, Vladimir."

He perceived a slight motion of her head as if she wanted to check the time on her wristwatch, but then thought better of it. On purpose, he'd let her wait for exactly ten minutes, since in his experience people unconsciously assumed the one showing up last held all the trump cards, even when that couldn't be further from the truth.

"Do you want to take a walk?" he asked as he noticed her shivering in the cold air. She nodded gratefully, which added another plus point for him. They walked a few minutes in silence, almost like lovers on a tryst, before he asked, "What did you want to tell me?"

"I might have the possibility of contacting my father."

He had expected as much. "And?"

"I want something in return." She said it in such a defiant tone he stopped in his tracks to look at her, his admiration for this woman growing.

"Tell me." He wouldn't make any promises, but if her request was reasonable, his superiors would surely acquiesce.

"Do you know about the American pilot, Glenn Davidson, who crashed in your territory?" She stared straight into his eyes, as if she could see the truth in them, but he was a master at deception and kept his expression completely blank, despite the shock.

There was no logical reason for her to be interested in that man and a horrible suspicion formed in his head. The Americans had sent her. This was a trap. He scanned his surroundings but couldn't see anyone. In his mind he retreated every step back to the car, but didn't come up with anything unusual. He was sure he hadn't been followed.

"Have you?" she insisted.

He wanted to slap himself for showing insecurity. "Oh yes. Now I remember. It was on the news. I believe he is severely injured but our doctors are giving him the best care available."

In a very unusual move, she took his hand between hers, drawing him nearer and whispering in his ear, "I want him returned to the American authorities alive. Then I'll give you my father."

He stumbled backward at the brazen demand. Who did she think she was, placing her conditions like that? "This is not in my power to do."

Disappointment crossed her beautiful face, but the next moment, she pursed her lips, dropped his hand and slowly turned away, while saying off-handedly. "I knew it was a waste of time to ask you. I should have talked to Captain Grusow from the NKVD right away, since he actually does have authority and doesn't only sweet-talk."

The monster of his uncontrollable rage reared its ugly head, making him see red. This woman dared call him a sweet-talking loser? She'd see how that would serve her. Insinuating she'd rather negotiate with the lousy rats over at NKVD! The bitch should be shaking in fear and not walking away from him. He put a heavy hand on her shoulder, squeezing just hard enough to make her realize that he held all the strings in his hand.

But she merely glared at him and said in the softest voice, "Oh, Vladi, are you really going to attack me smack-dab in the middle of the American zone, in a town that is crawling with their military? Don't you think they would be all too glad to get their hands on someone like you?"

He released the grip, painfully aware that he had grossly underestimated her – again. "I'm sorry. Please don't walk away."

She cocked her head. "I called you because you gave me the impression you hold enough power to negotiate a deal, but it looks like I was wrong. Whom do I need to talk to then? General Sokolov perhaps?"

That woman was flaming mad if she thought she could talk to the general.

"Why are you so interested in that pilot?" Vladi put on a conciliatory tone.

"Let's just say I owe him."

His jaw dropped to the floor when the truth hit him. Suddenly her motives became clear as crystal, because there was only one thing stronger than hate or fear. One thing that propelled her to brave the Soviets she so despised.

"You're in love with him!"

"I may be. Alright, I am." She put out her lower lip and he

would have told her how much he admired her guts if it weren't detrimental to his mission.

"Are you going to help me?" she insisted.

Noticing how she shivered in the cold, he suggested instead, "Let's go to my car and drive around. Then we can talk in the warmth."

She cast him a suspicious glance, before she nodded. "If you abduct me, you'll never get my father...and what he has to offer."

"He has an offer?"

"Let's talk in the car." Her smile showed him how much she enjoyed being the one in control...and that she knew how much he hated it, which made him hate it even more.

If she were a man, he'd gladly punch that smug grin from her face. But since she wasn't, he resigned himself to walking to the car in silence, where he deliberately didn't open the passenger door for her, started the motor before she'd even settled in the passenger seat, and yanked up the heating to maximum.

He drove out of the city, passing the airport with its bright lights and the constant humming of aircraft. *Bloody Americans!* He didn't want to imagine Stalin's wrath if they somehow licked the traffic controls and managed to keep the city supplied over winter. Things had looked bleak since they finished this darn Tegel Airport. Before the bad weather spell started, their daily tonnage had reached ten thousand tons, a number every expert on the face of the earth had deemed impossible less than three months ago.

Getting angry, he swiped all stray thoughts away and focused entirely on the situation at hand. "Your father has contacted you."

"He has." Zara paused for a moment and then looked at him. "I'll be frank. He wants me to help him cut a deal with the Americans."

Vladi gasped.

"He claims to have something they dearly want and he's willing to give it to them in exchange for immunity."

"What is it?" This information brought an unexpected turn and Vladi's mind was running wild considering possible implications. If the Americans wanted what Ulbert had to offer badly enough to cut him a deal, the Central Committee would surely want it too. Vladi might even be considered for the distinction "Hero of the Soviet Union", the highest honor in the country.

"I don't know."

It was getting warm in the car and as he glanced over to her side, her shivering had stopped.

"Even if you knew you wouldn't tell me, am I right?"

She smiled. "Maybe. It has something to do with art."

"Stolen art."

"Possibly."

There was something he'd not been able to understand. "Why are you willing to give up your father for that lover of yours?"

She sighed and didn't answer, but he wouldn't let her off the hook and waited patiently. The tension in the small car thickened to a point where he thought he could cut through it with the knife in his pocket. He leaned back, holding his hands leisurely on the steering wheel. At some point she would break and tell him.

"I hate him," she finally said.

"But you didn't blow the whistle on him."

"No. For all I care, he can rot in hell for his sins. But he's family after all, so I told him to get lost. Even he doesn't deserve the treatment your thugs will dole out." She pushed out her chin in defiance.

"What made you change your mind?" Vladi pondered whether he could recruit her to work for him. She'd make a fantastic undercover agent. Maybe later, when all of this was over and done with.

"I want Captain Davidson back. Unharmed."

"You know that General LeMay is on the matter already? Why do you think you can achieve more than him?"

She giggled. "Because he has to wade through tons of red tape and I don't."

He nodded. She was clever. "I'll have to talk to a few people."

"How fast can you do it?"

That was the problem. Propov was in a retreat with Stalin and nobody knew how long that would last. Vladi's boss might return to Berlin the next morning or five days from now. But Zara certainly wouldn't wait five days. She'd rather try her luck with the NKVD wastrel Grusow. *Over my dead body!* He wouldn't let this useless prick get away with such a big prize.

"How fast can you get your father?"

"Tomorrow night. But you'll only get him if Captain Davidson is alive and well."

"He's not well...he's sustained serious injuries during the crash."

"I'll settle for alive, conscious and in a condition that hasn't been worsened at the hands of your thugs."

Vladi's blood threatened to boil again, but he calmed himself, pretending she had meant the NKVD, who truly were stupid, nasty thugs.

"It's a deal." His mind was shifting into high gear. If Propov wasn't available, he had to pull the thing off by himself. Maybe it was for the best. A plan began to form in his mind. "How do you intend to get your father to give himself up to us instead of the Americans?"

"He doesn't have to know."

Vladi blinked several times. "Very sly."

"I learned a few things by watching you."

He had to laugh. "Are you sure you don't want to work for us? You would have a fantastic career."

"Certainly not. After this is over, I hope never to meet a Russian again in my entire life."

He couldn't hold it against her. "We'll use the green border. Come alone. You and your father. I'll be there with your friend and nobody will ever be the wiser."

"But how do we explain his sudden appearance?"

"Tell everyone he escaped with the help of an anonymous German sympathizer." Vladi drummed his fingers on the steering wheel. He couldn't have wished for a better opportunity to make the NKVD pay for their constant interference in Army intelligence business.

After the exchange was done, he would reap the rewards of capturing Ulbert, while the NKVD idiots would have to explain themselves for letting Davidson escape.

34

GLENN

Glenn woke up feeling slightly better, although most of his body was aching. He half-opened one eye, scanning the room for the NKVD men who'd visited him last night.

They had been very clear. If he didn't spill the beans about the inner workings of Operation Vittles, they'd resort to less conventional methods of interrogation. Once they started, he could never be released to his people, because it would cause a nasty diplomatic situation.

Naturally they hadn't used these exact words, but he'd understood them loud and clear: if he didn't talk, they'd torture him until he did and then dispose of him. He was scared to death, although foremost on his mind was Zara. The prospect of never seeing her again broke his heart. If only he'd told her how much he loved her before embarking on this accursed flight.

Around noon, the man who'd called himself Vladi entered his room. He looked the worse for wear, as if he hadn't slept all night, although he'd changed into an ill-fitting smart suit and brown shoes in place of his leather boots. Glenn wondered briefly if Vladi was the one designated to torture him.

"I'm here to propose a deal," Vladi said. "Your girlfriend—"

"Don't you dare drag her into this!" Glenn blurted out, and all but jumped off his bed.

The other man showed an infuriating smirk. "It's mutual, then. You know that love really can move mountains?"

Glenn heaved himself into a sitting position, his cracked ribs killing him, but he'd do anything to wipe the smug grin from Vladi's face. "If you laid as much as a finger on her, I'll kill you."

Vladi stopped him with a wave of his hand. "On the contrary, she sent me here. Do exactly as I say and you're back home with her by tonight."

Glenn scrutinized Vladi's blank expression. This had to be a trap. There was no chance in hell Zara was acquainted with this renegade and even less probability that she had sent him to Glenn. Weighing his options, he decided to play along.

"What exactly do you want me to do?"

"You talked to the NKVD?"

"I did, they were quite convincing." Glenn groaned at the memory of their conversation, which had ended with an unveiled threat, leaving very little to his imagination of what awaited him, should he not cooperate fully. Vladi's appearance, though, might be part of the game. A carrot and a stick.

Vladi chuckled. "An interesting way to put it. But back to us. I have an axe to grind with them and am therefore willing to help you escape."

"Escape? You're serious? And what about Zara?"

"We can talk about this in the car, but now we have to leave. Can you walk?"

"I guess." Glenn grimaced. He still wasn't sure whether he could trust Vladi. His mind raced, coming up with a million buts, but in the end, he decided to jump at the opportunity, however flimsy, incredible and outlandish it was, since the alternative was worse.

"Here." Vladi tossed him a brown shirt and black pants. "Get dressed."

Glenn involuntarily groaned when he pulled the hospital gown from his shoulders. Gritting his teeth, he bent forward to pick up the button-down shirt and somehow managed to squeeze his arms into the sleeves, despite the muscles in his battered body screaming with pain. Once he was done, he picked up the pants, but couldn't bend down enough to pull them over his feet.

"For God's Sake, am I supposed to dress you like a baby?" Vladi muttered and approached to help him into the pants and shoes. It was quite an embarrassing situation, alleviated only by the fear that someone might come through the door and find them out.

"Let's go!" Vladi hissed and slung his arm around Glenn's waist to keep him from stumbling. As fast as Glenn could manage, they rushed down the long hospital corridors that lay deserted in the siesta, when patients were supposed to sleep after lunch.

Glenn's eyes widened in shock when they came to a staircase. Somehow Vladi dragged him down the two floors. Hissing like a steam engine Glenn gathered every last morsel of energy he possessed, and the adrenaline pumping through his veins did the rest. Following Vladi's orders, he straightened his spine and walked as confidently as possible to the black car with civilian number plates that stood on the parking lot.

When he reached it, his legs were ready to give out under him and every muscle in his body was screaming with pain. Vladi settled in the driver's seat, opened the passenger door and dragged Glenn inside, before he started the motor and took off.

With some difficulty, Glenn moved his head to look back at the hospital. Nobody was following them.

"With some luck they won't notice your absence for the next two to three hours and by then you're already in safety." Vladi veered onto the Autobahn, and Glenn's spirits lifted when he realized they were indeed driving westward. Since he'd decided to put his life into Vladi's hands, he might as well enjoy the ride.

"Why are you doing this?" Glenn turned his head and peered curiously at the other man.

Vladi drummed his hands onto the steering wheel. "Let's just say I have some scores to settle. And your girlfriend can be very convincing."

"How do you know her?" Glenn didn't like the fact that Zara and Vladi seemed to be friends, because that man wasn't someone his sweet girl should spend time with.

"We had a brief encounter before she moved to the American zone." For some reason, the thought that they might have been a couple stabbed at Glenn's heart. He forced the thought aside and clasped his hands around the door handle so hard, his knuckles became white. He couldn't expect that she'd never had a boyfriend before him...although he sure wished she hadn't.

Vladi glanced over at him and stated, "You're jealous."

"I'm not." This man was unnerving. Never in his life would he have expected such a brute to be so perceptive.

"You have no reason to be. Our encounter was purely business and not very pleasant."

Glenn's blood ran hot. "I'll break every bone in your damn body if I ever find out that you hurt her..."

"Save your breath. I'd never harm a woman." A long silence ensued, before Vladi continued. "She seems so fragile and soft, but I swear underneath her sweet exterior that woman is made of steel. She annoyed the hell out of me."

Glenn suppressed a chuckle. "You're not the only one. Once she is determined to do something, not even a tank can stop her."

"Tell me. I severely underestimated her. You're a lucky guy. Without her intervention you'd soon go through the wringer to spill your secrets."

Glenn bit his lip. He knew all too well what he'd escaped from. "What is she? Some kind of super spy?"

Vladi laughed out loud. "Nothing of that sort. On the contrary, she told me to go to hell, when I asked her to work for us."

"Who exactly is 'us'?" Glenn probed. He was sure he wouldn't get a satisfying answer, but one could try.

"Let's talk about how this is going to happen," Vladi said instead of answering the question. "I'm taking a huge risk and I need you to do exactly as I say."

Glenn nodded his approval.

"We'll leave the Autobahn just before the zonal border and drive to our designated meeting spot. Zara has required that you be in good shape, so you'll have to walk over to her to prove it. She'll be there with a man and you need to convince him to come with you to my car."

"Why would I do that?"

"Because in your current condition you're no match for me and because of this." He pointed to the revolver peeking out from under his jacket. "Make him believe you're a negotiator for the Americans, say yes to everything he wants and tell him that the person in charge, me, is waiting for him at the car. Once I have the man, you're free to go."

Glenn's jaw hung agape. A million questions were storming into his brain, still under the influence of pain-killers and not working at its usual speed. "Who is this man?"

"A war criminal. SS-Obersturmführer, high up in the concentration camp hierarchy."

"I'm being exchanged for a war criminal?" Glenn didn't know whether he should be flattered or annoyed.

"Exactly. We want to put him on trial."

"I'm sure my people want to do the same, if he really is who you say," Glenn argued.

"See, then there's no reason for you not to help me. He'll receive his righteous punishment, just not at your hands, but at ours. What's the difference?"

Glenn thought for a while. It didn't make much of a difference. This Nazi, whoever he was, deserved whatever fate the Soviets had in store for him. Should Glenn feel sorry for an SS-Obersturmführer who might have to face many years hard labor in a gulag? He decided that he should not. Nobody had climbed the SS career ladder without dirtying his hands.

"Does anyone know about this exchange?"

Vladi shook his head.

"Then, what are my guarantees that you won't shoot me once you have the Nazi?"

"None."

"At least you're honest." Glenn couldn't help but admire the other man for his guts. Despite his appearance he seemed to be trustworthy. Not that Glenn had many options. After a long silence he asked, "What's in it for you?"

"Fame and fortune."

"Who is the man Zara is exchanging for me?"

"That, you should ask her yourself."

Glenn didn't ask further questions, since Vladi wouldn't answer anyway and decided to feel flattered at Zara's scheming to get him home. It was slightly embarrassing that his freedom depended on the actions of a woman, but the wave of love coursing through his veins pushed the awkward feeling aside.

35

ZARA

The next morning, as soon as Cath had left the house, Zara picked up the shopping basket and walked to the grocery store. But first, she passed by the bakery and asked for Josef Heindel. The baker's woman didn't seem surprised and told her where Zara could find him.

Zara bought the groceries, went home, dusted the house and then prepared herself a quick lunch before she left to meet her father. Her heart was thumping up her throat, while she was trying to maintain a calm exterior. She'd been reflecting on her actions over and over again. Despite the fact that her father was a beast and deserved punishment, she hated herself for being the one to hand him over.

Doubts crept into her heart and the betrayal against her own blood weighed heavily on her soul. Turning him in to his certain conviction and subsequent execution felt like taking a sword into her own hands and slashing his throat. She shrieked and jumped aside when she saw a puddle of blood on the sidewalk. Holding a hand over her heart, she blinked a few times, taking a deep breath.

Muddied water.

She swallowed down the lump forming in her throat, afraid God was punishing her for this frivolous act of throwing her father to the wolves to rescue a man she'd known for a few short months. Glancing at the phone booth further down the street she longed to rush into it and call Vladi to cancel the entire operation.

But that wouldn't help, since Vladi must already be on his way to the agreed meeting point near Fulda. Her steps slowed down the nearer she got to the indicated address, until thoughts of Glenn spurred her on. Vladi had verified her greatest fears that Glenn would not leave the Soviet zone alive if he didn't willingly tell them everything he knew. Knowing Glenn, she was sure he wouldn't cooperate.

She had to do this. A bad man in exchange for a good one. It felt like betrayal, and it probably was, but it was her only chance to get Glenn back. She closed her eyes for a moment, willing away the happy thoughts of her childhood, and focusing on the horrible ones instead. Indulging his family on Christmas didn't make her father a good man, neither did kissing her knee when she'd fallen and scratched it. Nothing good and caring he'd ever done could offset the crime of sending thousands to their deaths after months and years of the most terrible suffering.

She was doing the right thing. Yes, she was.

Even before she knocked at the door, her father opened with a satisfied expression on his face. "I knew you would change your mind."

"Good afternoon to you too," she responded, ready to add a scathing remark, but thought better of it. Glenn's life depended on her father's cooperation and therefore she had to play nice. "I have talked with the Americans, as you wished."

"And? Are they willing to negotiate?" His face was eager, anxious even. Her next words would be crucial in lulling him into a sense of security.

"They are very interested..." She had thought of a thousand ways to best tackle this point without raising his suspicions. "... but they want more details about the kind of art you mentioned."

"Do they think me stupid? I'm not going to spill the beans before I have a written paper in my hands granting me immunity."

She had expected this response. "That's what I told them."

"And... what did they suggest?"

"Meeting directly with the man in charge of the recovery of stolen artifacts. He has the power to grant you immunity if what you offer is really as huge as you say." Zara was walking on thin ice here, since she had no idea if such a department even existed. It had been Vladi's idea; he'd argued that if the Soviets had a unit like this, the Americans must have one, too.

"At last these upstarts show some common sense. Who is the man? Snyder?"

Zara's blood froze in her veins, but she managed to keep calm and say, "I'm sorry, I don't know." Looking at the suspicious expression on her father's face, she improvised. "Captain Davidson is my liaison—"

"A captain?" her father pouted. "I need to talk at least to a general. This is a huge thing."

"I know." Vladi had warned her this might happen. Her father wasn't stupid and if he wanted to make a deal — whatever valuable thing he had in exchange for his freedom — he'd only talk to the top brass.

"This has to be done under the utmost secrecy, until the deal is official. This is why we will meet with Captain Davidson, who then will arrange for you to meet his boss."

"Let's go, then." Her father stepped out of the door, the knob in his hand.

"Wait."

"What?"

"We have to go to a town near Fulda."

His expression changed from confident to bewildered. "You're keeping something from me. Tell me! And don't you dare lie! What are those blockheads up to?"

Years ago, Zara would have stood shuddering in front of him, unable to defy his commands, but not anymore. She straightened her shoulders, and stared right back at her father. "You cannot be seen near the airbase, or some overzealous MP might recognize you, leak your appearance to the press and there won't be a deal. The Americans don't want to risk a public propaganda disaster by appearing to sacrifice justice for material benefit."

"That makes sense. They're cleverer than I gave them credit for. Maybe not the brutish gangsters we always pegged them as."

Zara forced a smile on her lips. She didn't want to argue with her father, for fear he'd get upset and rush off. She only had one chance at getting this right. Vladi had chosen Fulda, or better Nüsttal, a small village nearby, because it was located at the "green border" between the Eastern and Western zones of the country, and Vladi's choice for crossing over.

"We're taking my car," her father suddenly said.

"You have a car?" Zara's eyes all but popped out. Her father had always been a car lover and had owned quite the motor pool of beautiful and elegant Mercedes-Benz limousines, as well as more practical staff cars by Volkswagen, but Zara had never once entertained the idea that even as a criminal in hiding he had access to a car. She gathered that he must have many powerful former Nazi friends in high positions in Germany.

"SILLY GIRL. Of course I have a car. Or do you expect me to use the train?"

Actually that was exactly how she'd planned on getting them to Nüsttal. Bile rose in her throat. Most of those Nazis were atrocious criminals like her father, but too many had made a similar deal with the occupiers who needed them for one reason or another, and now held positions of power as if the war and capitulation had never happened.

As much as she hated the Soviets, she had to give them credit for relentlessly purging former Nazis from the ranks, albeit catching many innocents in their net, too.

The drive to Nüsttal took two hours and darkness began to fall over the land. Zara had never liked the winter months when the daylight seemed to last not much longer than the blink of an eye. But right now, she welcomed the night that would make her deceit easier.

Vladi had told her about a villa that stood directly on the demarcation line, and since it was disputed to whom it belonged, none of the Allies used the building and it had been given over to slow decay. It presented the perfect backdrop to their handover.

"My friends can help you," her father said.

Zara had been distracted by her worries and didn't know what she needed help with. "What can they do?"

"You're a stupid girl!" he scolded her, chipping away at any fondness she might still hold for him. "My daughter doesn't have to work as a servant for some obscure lowbrow whose grandparents were still sitting on trees."

"It's good work."

"No, it's not! It's beneath your dignity! I didn't send you to higher education for this. Lothar is willing to marry you."

"What?" She jerked her head around and stared at him, aghast. Lothar was one of her father's closest friends – and about the same age. Did he actually expect her to marry some old Nazi twice her age? Of course he did, and it wasn't the first time either.

"Yes, really." He patted her leg in the same condescending way he'd done when she was a child. Everything in her rebelled against his touch, before he even uttered his next words: "Think about it. He's a judge at the high court and can offer you a life in luxury."

Never in her life would she acquiesce to this outrageous request, but she thought it better to remain silent.

"There's the Fulda exit," she said and unfolded a hand-written map with directions from Vladi. "From here it's about ten minutes to Nüsttal."

36

GLENN

"We have arrived," Vladi said as he parked the car in front of a villa of decaying beauty.

"Here?" Glenn tried to keep the surprise out of his voice. The house stood at the end of a long winding road leading from the main street. It stood proud amidst a small copse of trees and plenty of empty fields. Then it dawned on him. "No joke. We're going across the green border."

"What did you expect? A red carpet?" Vladi stepped out of the car and produced Glenn's uniform jacket and field cap from the trunk. "Better wear this."

"Just to get this clear, what we're doing here isn't approved by either side?"

Vladi shrugged.

For a second, Glenn pondered whether he should take part in this rogue operation. But with the alternatives being torture and death at the hospital or a bullet in his back while trying to run away, he decided it wasn't worth it to fret over legalities.

"And this has been Zara's idea?"

"Brazen woman. Would love to have her on my team, but

she's made her bed with the imperialists," Vladi said with a salacious tone.

Despite the insult, Glenn's entire body warmed at the certainty that Zara was doing this to rescue him. He'd set his cap for her from the moment of their first meeting, but if he were honest, in the beginning he'd been more interested in the thrill of the chase and hadn't expected her to weasel herself into his heart.

"Don't forget to play your role," Vladi warned him. "If anything goes wrong, I shoot her first, and then you. Understood?"

Glenn looked into Vladi's blue eyes, recognizing the glimmer of unwavering determination. It was clear that Vladi would make good on his threat, and they wouldn't be the first persons he'd killed in cold blood, either. A slight tremble ran though his limbs, before training and adrenaline took over and stilled his body, while alerting his brain. He'd be damned if he did anything to endanger Zara. "No need to worry. I'll stick exactly to your plan."

"Good man. It would be a shame to kill you, because I actually grew fond of you both."

"Is that a compliment?" Glenn felt the same way. Despite having different beliefs and being on opposite sides of the unfolding Cold War, he shared many character traits with Vladi and respected him.

"It's the best you'll ever get from me."

Glenn stretched his hurting leg, put on his surprisingly undamaged uniform and walked in the direction Vladi had indicated. At first, he didn't see anything, but then two persons stepped out from the copse of trees. Despite the darkness he recognized Zara. Her pale skin gleamed in the moonlight and her long dark hair rustled in the breeze like a wafting flag.

The person next to her was slightly smaller, but with a stronger build. He must be the Obersturmführer. Fear gripped

Glenn's heart. If the man suspected something, he might use Zara as a hostage, or Vladi might shoot her. Taking a deep breath, he resigned himself to going through with the plan and hoping for the best.

Vividly sensing the presence of the gun Vladi was training at his back, Glenn walked forward until he came to a standstill in front of Zara and the man whose facial features looked surprisingly similar to hers.

"Captain Davidson?" the Obersturmführer said. "I'm sure my daughter has told you that I have extremely valuable information and am willing to give it up in exchange for immunity."

Glenn winced. *Daughter? This is her father? Good god!* She was willing to hand her own father over to the Soviets? For him?

"Yes. I'm not the one to negotiate the deal, but I'll bring you to General Snyder if you would follow me."

"General Snyder. At last someone with sense," Ulbert remarked and stepped forward.

Glenn suddenly was in a hurry to get away from Zara and willed her with his thoughts to take herself into safety, which, of course, she didn't.

"Isn't my daughter coming with us?" Ulbert asked.

"I'm sorry, my orders were limited to you."

Ulbert stared at him, suspicion appearing in his eyes and said, "I'm not going anywhere without her."

Glenn shrugged. Should Vladi solve this problem. "If you insist, she can certainly come with us." The three of them walked toward the entrance of the house, and Glenn prayed that Ulbert wouldn't notice it was abandoned before it was too late. Just as they reached the stairs leading up to the entrance gate, Vladi, who'd been hiding behind a marble statue, ambushed their group and knocked Ulbert out.

"Well done." Vladi said and turned toward Zara, "It was a

pleasure working with you. Anytime again, you know how to reach me."

Zara glared at him, "You can wait until kingdom come. I'm done with your lot!"

"See, I told you it's best not to tangle with her." Vladi addressed Glenn. "But thanks anyway. You two are free to go. So long!" With these words he grabbed Ulbert's limp body and threw it over his shoulder.

Glenn stared after him until he entered the car and drove away. Only then did he turn around to wrap Zara in his arms. "Thank you."

"I was so scared I'd never see you again," she whispered, before she shyly looked up at him and gave him that wonderful smile of hers that always warmed his insides. The tension between them began to boil and he sensed that something had shifted, something wonderful.

He pressed his lips on hers, exploring her soft mouth. Together they stood, oblivious to the cold air, and the world around them, relishing the overwhelming emotion of seeing each other again. Glenn never wanted this kiss to end, but his battered body reminded him of reality and he came up for air. "And now?"

"Now what?" Zara stared at him, slightly breathless. The sweetest hue of pink shaded her cheeks and he wished to kiss her all over again, but that had to wait for later.

"We need to get away from here."

"Oh, yes…" She was worrying her lower lip, all the strength and courage fleeing her body. "…I hadn't thought about that. We go home?"

"How?"

New spirit returned into her eyes as she explained, "My father's car. He parked it behind that copse."

Once again, he felt warmth surge through his body. When all of this was over, he must ask her why she had decided to sacrifice a family member for him – the man she pretended not to love.

On the short distance to the car across uneven ground, the increasing pain in his leg and ribs almost killed him and he breathed with relief when they had reached their destination. He opened the passenger door and fell onto the seat, carefully grabbing his injured leg with both hands to heave it inside when he looked up into Zara's shocked eyes.

"What are you doing?" she said.

"What do you mean? Didn't you say we use this car?"

"Yes, but..." Once again, she worried her lower lip. "...I can't drive."

"You can't drive?"

"No. My father thought it inappropriate for a girl and after the war...I mean who owns a car nowadays?"

Glenn groaned. Even the thought of bending his knee to press down the clutch sent painful stabs through his leg. He leaned back to think, but there was no way around it. "I guess I'll have to drive then. But I'll never make it back to Wiesbaden."

"I'm sorry," Zara whispered as soon as he squeezed himself behind the wheel with a pained grimace.

"Whatever are you sorry for? For rescuing me?"

"No, for not thinking this through."

He captured her fidgeting hands with his and held them still. "You saved my life, so I'm not picky about the circumstances, since it could be so much worse." Relief showed on her face. "But you're right, we need a plan. Even if I could drive us all the way to Wiesbaden, how would we explain all of this, since I assume nobody approved of your little exchange mission."

She clasped a hand in front of her mouth. "Nobody can know, or Vladi will get into a whole lot of trouble."

Jealousy snaked up in his bones at her concern for the

Soviet, despite realizing she was right. Vladi had taken on a risk by helping Glenn escape and it was only just that he would get his reward in return. "You're right. He told me to say a sympathetic East German helped me."

"But how?"

By now, his brain was running more or less with normal speed again and he thought of the best way to keep both Vladi and Zara out of this. As much as he hated to lie to his superiors, it had to be done. "Let that be my problem. I'll drive you to the train station, we leave the car there and while you catch a train back home, I'll find my way to the army barracks."

She squeezed his hands. "It's only a ten-minute drive to Fulda, and your people have a huge garrison stationed there."

Glenn desperately wanted to lean over to give her a kiss, but atrocious pain was searing his ribs as he tried to turn his upper body. Instead, he pulled her hand to his mouth and pressed his lips on it, before saying, "Let's go then."

37

VLADI

Two weeks later

Everything had worked according to plan. Vladi had elegantly put the blame for Captain Davidson's escape on the NKVD idiots who couldn't even guard an injured man while Vladi himself had been working diligently to capture a war criminal.

As predicted, his superiors all the way up to General Sokolov had been over the moon about the capture of SS-Ober-sturmführer Ulbert and had promoted Vladi to the rank of Major, which gave him a whole new array of *pajok*, gifts the Central Committee gave to deserved functionaries. One of the major perks was that he was about to move out of the barracks at Karlshorst and into an apartment of his own.

Now he had only one more task to complete. When those bastard French had blasted the Soviet radio towers located next to the new Tegel Airport a while ago, claiming they presented a risk for the air traffic, General Sokolov had thrown a fit. And somehow, Vladi had been made responsible for not preventing the construction of Tegel Airport. To save his neck, he'd boldly offered to arrange the tragic accident of Victor Richards, the American soldier who'd been the head engineer for Tegel.

But since the French, Americans, and British had basically closed their sectors in Berlin to Soviet military, it had been increasingly difficult to plan anything and Vladi was running out of time, because Richards was earmarked to return to Wiesbaden by the end of the year.

Coincidence helped Vladi out, when he met with one of his best tipsters.

38

ZARA

Zara was dusting the library when the door rang. Wondering who'd visit at this time of the morning, she walked to the door and opened it to a beaming Glenn with a huge bouquet of flowers in his hands.

Her heart did a double dip. She hadn't seen him since Fulda, because first he'd been at the military hospital and then quarantined for debriefing or however they called it.

"Glenn. You're here." Her brain went blissfully blank as she sank into his arms.

He pushed her inside the house and knocked the door close with his foot, before kissing her like a drowning man gasping for air, the flowers floating to the floor. Only when they had to come up for breath did she disentangle herself from his embrace and bend down to pick up the flowers. "Are these for me?"

"Yes, I'm sorry." He looked at her with that charming smile she'd missed so much. "When I saw you, I forgot everything else."

"Come in. I'll put them into a vase." She walked to the

kitchen and he followed her, sitting down at the table. "Did they give you a hard time?"

"No. Just the usual. The doctors made me pass dozens of tests and declared me fit to fly again starting next week."

She knew he was purposely misunderstanding her question, but didn't press him. She arranged the flowers in the vase and then turned around to look at him. "I'm so happy to see you."

"Me too. And I wanted to ask if you'd like to come with me to Bob Hope's Christmas concert?"

"I'd love to." Her eyes spilled over. The Gardners and their friends had talked about nothing but the upcoming tour of this beloved comedian to entertain the troops who had to spend Christmas far away from their families. Tickets for the show in the Wiesbaden Opera House had become coveted treasures.

"Unfortunately, I couldn't get tickets for the show in Wiesbaden." His eyes twinkled with mischief. "But for Berlin."

"What? I can't go to Berlin..." She stopped when she saw him laughing heartily. "What kind of shenanigans have you planned?"

"Nothing. I promise. But I whined and complained to my superiors until they allowed me a twenty-four-hour stay in Berlin to see the concert, and to bring one passenger with me."

"With you?" Zara was dumbstruck. "How?"

"On the aircraft."

"But civilians can't travel on your planes."

"Sometimes they can. We make exceptions for journalists or dignitaries."

"I'm neither."

He laughed again and pulled her onto his lap. "In your case you get a permit, because you are very important to me."

She looked at him, suspiciously. "Are you serious? Your superiors will allow this?"

"Yes. But just this one time and you have to find your own accommodation in Berlin."

"That's not a problem. I'll send a letter to Marlene right away..." She jumped from his lap to go to the library and take a sheet of paper, but he caught her before she even reached the door. "Is that a yes?"

"Of course it's a yes. Do you actually believe I would forego seeing Bob Hope live?" she teased him and took delight at his dismayed face.

"First Andy Williams, then this Soviet soldier and now Bob Hope...are there any more men in your life I should know about?" He'd said it in a light, teasing tone, but his eyes turned serious.

She shook her head. "I would go anywhere just to see you. I guess I never told you, but the days after your crash were horrible. I couldn't sleep, couldn't work, couldn't do anything...it was then that I realized I love you."

"I love you too," he said and followed up his words with a kiss so passionate, her entire body tingled.

On Christmas day, Zara arrived in Berlin as a passenger on Glenn's aircraft. She was giddy with anticipation not only to watch the Bob Hope concert, but also to meet her friends Bruni and Marlene.

Strictly speaking, the show was only for the American troops, but Victor Richards, Bruni's newest lover, had managed to get tickets for both Bruni and Marlene.

Zara spotted Bruni's platinum blonde mane and rushed toward the small group, embracing both of the women at once. "Bruni, Marlene. I missed you so much!"

"We missed you too, how is life in Wiesbaden?" Marlene asked.

"Good, but how are you coping with the blockade?"

"Enduring." Bruni extricated herself from Zara's embrace and arranged her curls. "But it's no fun."

"I wish I could take you with me to Wiesbaden," Zara said.

"Leaving Berlin? Never!" Marlene and Bruni said in unison and all three of them began to laugh, until Zara noticed the handsome soldier with the dirty blond hair and the bright green-grey eyes standing a few feet behind them and looking slightly lost. She dimly remembered having met him at the farewell party Bruni had organized for her before leaving for Wiesbaden.

"That's your guy? What happened to your list?" she whispered. Bruni used to have a list of requirements for a man to go out with, and as far as Zara remembered, this guy had been a decisive "not suitable for a long-term relationship."

"To hell with lists." Much to Zara's surprise, Bruni's face lit up with unabated emotion as she turned around to grab Victor's hand. "This is Victor, my boyfriend. And this is Zara, one of my best friends. The one who moved to Wiesbaden just before Uncle Joe decided to strangle us all to death."

Victor stepped forward to shake Zara's hand and then wrapped his arm around Bruni's shoulder in the loving-possessive way of a man who was completely smitten. And, astonishingly, Bruni didn't protest. On the contrary, she leaned against him in the loving-snuggly way of a woman who'd fallen head over heels, which was completely out of character for Bruni.

"I'll tell you all about the lovebirds, later," Marlene teased and nodded at Glenn, who was standing behind Zara. "And who's this handsome man?"

Zara felt herself flush beet-red and was still struggling to find the right words when Glenn stepped forward, extended his hand to Marlene and said, "I'm Glenn," before he put his arm around Zara's waist in the same loving-possessive way she'd just observed on Victor with Bruni.

"We should really go inside, or we'll be too far in the back to see anything," Victor said and the small group moved inside the hangar.

Zara felt a slight panic rising in her throat when she was suddenly surrounded by nothing but uniforms, bad memories creeping up on her. Glenn must have sensed her distress, because he pressed her harder against him and whispered, "Relax. I'm here with you."

She reveled in how fast he'd learned to read her body language and how he always said or did the right thing to suppress her burgeoning panic.

The show was fantastic and despite not understanding all of Bob Hope's jokes, she couldn't remember a time she'd had more fun. The fact of being together with all the people she loved the most, filled her with happiness and she felt like a beaming light bulb all night.

After the show they went to one of the bars in the French sector. Bruni suggested a new and posh place next to the lake with the name Nieder Neuendorfer See, with supposedly the best drinks and music.

She was right, and it was already morning when Victor offered to drive everyone home. They stepped out of the bar, a thin blanket of freshly fallen snow covering the ground.

"You wait here with Glenn, while I get the jeep," Victor suggested with a glance at the high heels of the three women.

Zara was only too glad to agree, since she could barely keep her eyes open and her feet were hurting viciously from standing, walking and dancing in heels all night. Her glance fell on a half-track sitting on the curb with its motor running and she wondered what he was up to.

But the next moment, Glenn wrapped his arms around her and she leaned against him, feeling the warmth emanating from his body. She smiled at him and together they looked up into the sky, where an endless string of planes was lined up, shining like the brightest stars as they brought their life-saving supplies into the city.

In this very moment she was the happiest person on earth.

AUTHOR'S NOTES

Dear Reader,

Thank you so much for reading **In the Skies**. The Berlin Fractured series has taken me deep into the Cold War and it has been eye-opening to research how everything unfolded.

While **On the Brink** concentrated on the situation in Berlin and the construction of Tegel Airport, I wanted to explore the other end of the airlift in Wiesbaden/Frankfurt in this book. And who would be a better protagonist for this than a pilot who's actually flying that *Berlin thing*?

Glenn was mentioned as a side character in the previous book, and he was the natural choice. I took some liberties with his character for the sake of simplicity: he's a combination of several courageous men who experienced the anecdotes mentioned in this book. The coal dumps, the condom episode, the transport of millions of Deutsche Mark, the buzzing by Yaks, all are based upon eyewitness reports. And no airlift book could be complete without mentioning the candy parachutes and their inventor Gail Halvordsen.

I want to thank my reader Louise Nichols and her husband, who worked for the Canadian Airforce (although both are too young to have participated in the Berlin Airlift), for checking my flight scenes for plausibility. If despite this, not all technical details are accurate, I hope you'll be lenient with me.

In the beginning I was skeptical about Zara's personality, because she had not been very much present in the other two books, always hiding in the background. But once I pushed her into the limelight she redeemed herself quite nicely, I think. I'm especially glad that she got her happy ending and found true love with Glenn. The two of them will definitely appear in the next book of the series **Into the Unknown**, which has Bruni and Victor as main characters. Without giving any spoilers I can tell you that Victor will suffer an accident and has to be flown out to Wiesbaden. Bruni is going to move heaven and earth to be with him, which is not an easy task to do because of the ongoing blockade. Lots of research to do here!

Now on to my favorite villain: Vladi. I know I shouldn't but I completely fell in love with his bad boy attitude. It was fun to put him into all these struggles between believing about the benefits of communism and explaining away the violence and oppression of it.

The story line of Zara's kidnapping is completely fictional, but similar things have happened and the U-boot at Hohen-schönhausen is real. The infamous prison continued to exist throughout the Soviet occupation until the German reunifica-tion in 1989. Many regime critics were held there under inhuman conditions. The prison has now been turned into a museum. Unfortunately, I could only take the virtual tour due to everything being closed because of the coronavirus when I was in the final stages of writing this book.

But I did have a chance to visit the heritage-protected Tempelhof Airport during a visit to Berlin and found it truly amazing. As you can probably guess I was especially impressed by the existence of a bowling alley and a basketball court in the administration building. The basketball court, by the way, has recently been closed because of structural damage to the building originating from the bombings during WWII.

General Tunner is a real person and I have tried to depict him in the way he described himself in his memoir called **Over the Hump**, which I recommend to everyone interested in the airlift topic. Only a small part of his book is dedicated to the Berlin airlift, but it's an invaluable source to get an idea about the chaos during the first days and the awful conditions for the crews, especially the lack of proper accommodation, food, sleep, and aircraft.

Glenn's flight to Berlin on Black Friday, August 13, 1948 used General Tunner's experiences of this flight, as well as several eyewitness reports from crews who flew in the same block.

Buzzing occurred frequently – a total of 733 incidents were reported during the airlift, and at least one fatal accident happened. On November 18, 1948 a British Dakota returning from Berlin to Lübeck crashed and two crewmembers were killed, the other two survived heavily injured and were brought to a Soviet military hospital.

The part, though, where Glenn is kept at the hospital for interrogation and possible torture is completely fictional and I don't know whether this would have happened in real life or not.

Zara's exchanging her father with Vladi's help is also my own idea and I know of no case where this happened in reality. But then the people involved in the exchange all agreed to keep it a secret.

Thanks again for reading **In the Skies** and I would thoroughly appreciate it if you found the time to leave a review.

Marion Kummerow

ALSO BY MARION KUMMEROW

Love and Resistance in WW2 Germany

Unrelenting

Unyielding

Unwavering

War Girl Series

Downed over Germany (Prequel)

War Girl Ursula (Book 1)

War Girl Lotte (Book 2)

War Girl Anna (Book 3)

Reluctant Informer (Book 4)

Trouble Brewing (Book 5)

Fatal Encounter (Book 6)

Uncommon Sacrifice (Book 7)

Bitter Tears (Book 8)

Secrets Revealed (Book 9)

Together at Last (Book 10)

Endless Ordeal (Book 11)

Not Without My Sister (Spin-off)

Berlin Fractured

From the Ashes (Book 1)

On the Brink (Book 2)

In the Skies (Book 3)

Into the Unknown (Book 4)

A Jewess in Nazi Germany

Turning Point (Prequel)

A Light in the Window

From the Dark We Rise

Historical Romance

Second Chance at First Love

Find all my books here:

http://www.kummerow.info

CONTACT ME

I truly appreciate you taking the time to read (and enjoy) my books. And I'd be thrilled to hear from you!
If you'd like to get in touch with me you can do so via

Twitter:
http://twitter.com/MarionKummerow

Facebook:
http://www.facebook.com/AutorinKummerow

Website
http://www.kummerow.info

Made in the USA
Middletown, DE
22 May 2022

66086411R00151